THE LONELY COMMITTEE

WRITTEN BY Molly Muldoon

ILLUSTRATED & COLORS BY Kel McDonald

GIRLS' DAY

WRITTEN BY Annie Griggs ILLUSTRATED BY Abigail Starling

COLORS BY Andrew Dalhouse

HEEL TURN

WRITTEN BY Danielle Radford ILLUSTRATED BY Shadia Amin

COLORS BY Andrew Dalhouse

ALL PAGES LETTERED BY Crank!

COVER BY George Caltsoudas

Aggretsuko™
meet her world

ONI PRESS
AN ONI PRESS PUBLICATION

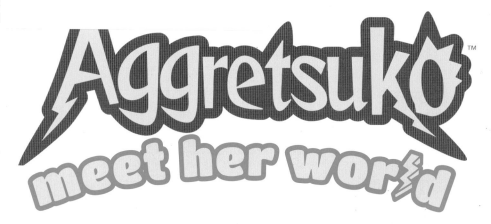

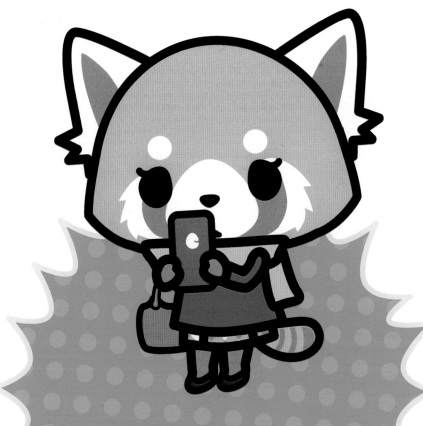

DESIGNED BY SARAH ROCKWELL   **EDITED BY** ROBERT MEYERS

SPECIAL THANKS TO
CINDY SUZUKI, JEFF PARKER, MARJORIE SANTOS, SUSAN ZHANG, SUSAN TRAN,
AND LINH FORSE FOR THEIR INVALUABLE ASSISTANCE.

onipress.com

@onipress

lionforge.com

@lionforge

PUBLISHED BY ONI-LION FORGE PUBLISHING GROUP, LLC
James Lucas Jones, president & publisher
Sarah Gaydos, editor in chief Charlie Chu,
e.v.p. of creative & business development
Alex Segura, s.v.p of marketing & sales Brad
Rooks, director of operations Amber O'Neill,
special projects manager Margot Wood,
director of marketing & sales Katie Sainz,
marketing manager Tara Lehmann, publicist
Holly Aitchison, consumer marketing manager
Troy Look, director of design & production
Kate Z. Stone, senior graphic designer Carey
Hall, graphic designer Sarah Rockwell,
graphic designer Hilary Thompson, graphic
designer Angie Knowles, digital prepress lead
Vincent Kukua, digital prepress technician
Jasmine Amiri, senior editor Shawna Gore,
senior editor Amanda Meadows, senior
editor Robert Meyers, senior editor, licensing
Desiree Rodriguez, editor Grace Scheipeter,
editor Zack Soto, editor Chris Cerasi, editorial
coordinator Steve Ellis, vice president of
games Ben Eisner, game developer Michelle
Nguyen, executive assistant Jung Lee, logistics
coordinator Kuian Kellum, warehouse assistant
Joe Nozemack, publisher emeritus

sanrio.com

 @sanrio

@aggretsuko

aggretsuko

@aggretsuko

aggretsuko

© 2021 SANRIO CO., LTD.
S/T·F
Used Under License.
www.sanrio.com

SIL-34865

First Edition: NOVEMBER 2021
ISBN 978-1-62010-979-3
eISBN 978-1-63715-032-0

Printing numbers:
1 3 5 7 9 10 8 6 4 2

Library of Congress Control Number 2021938023

Printed in China.

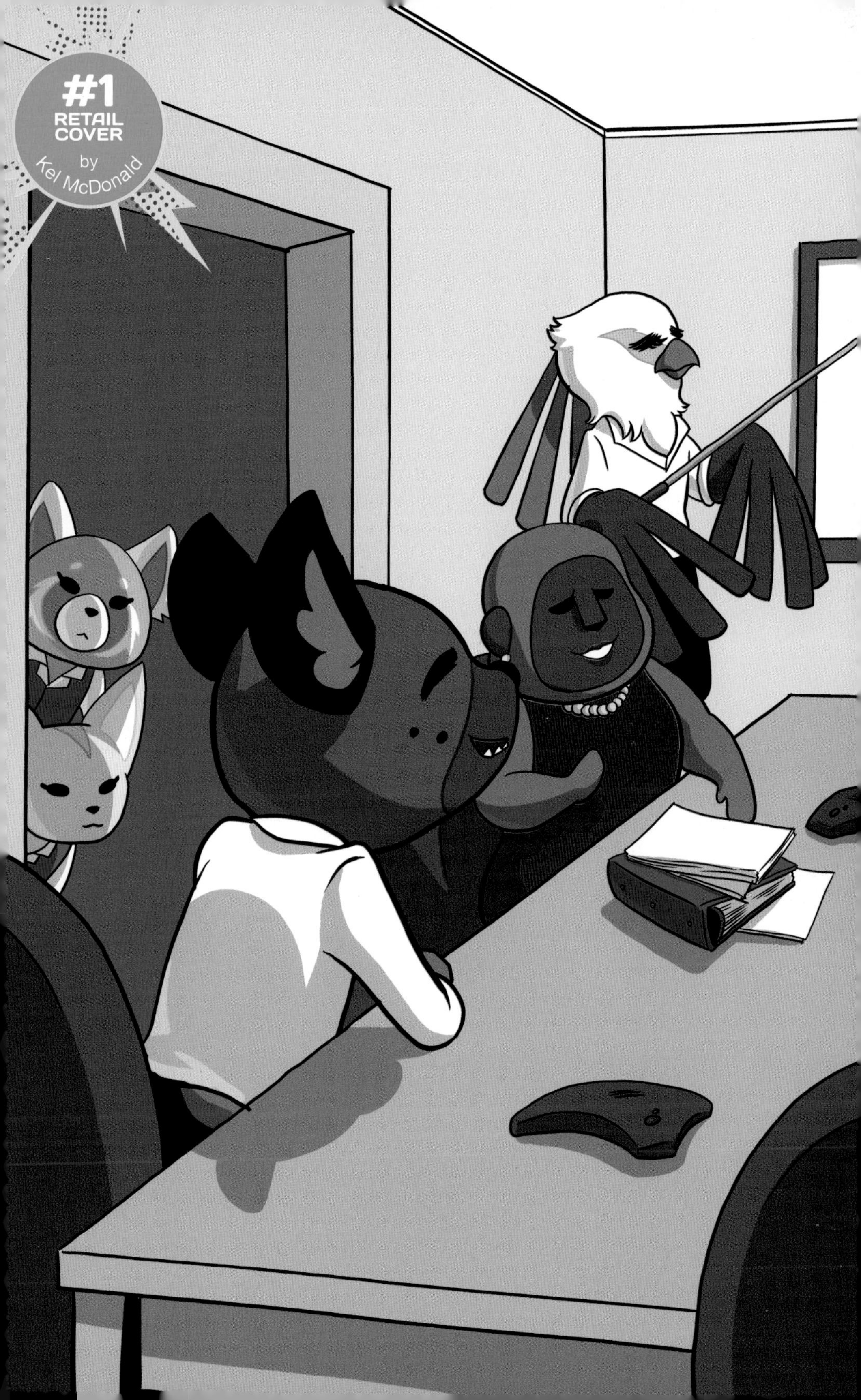
#1
RETAIL
COVER
by
Kel McDonald

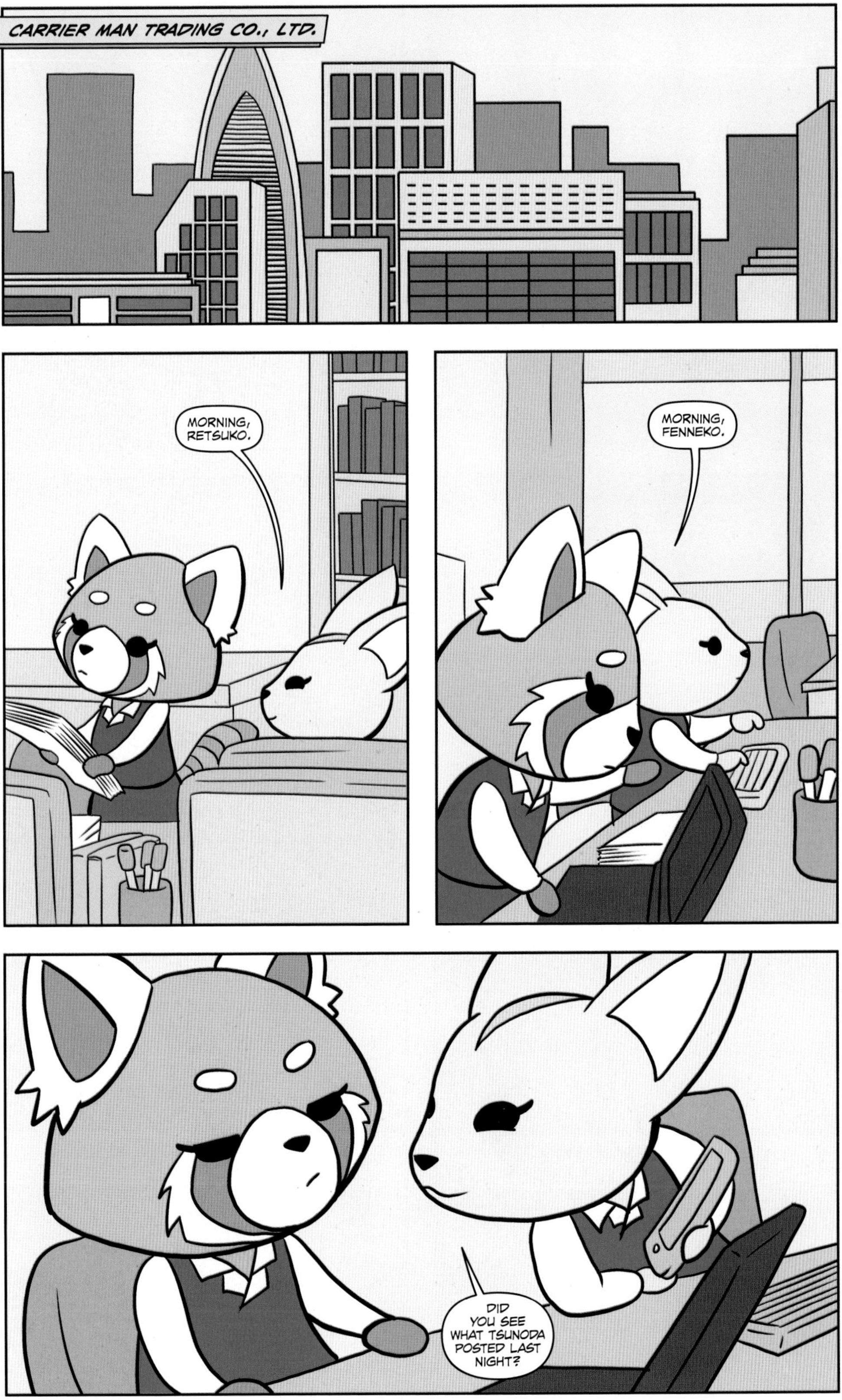
CARRIER MAN TRADING CO., LTD.
MORNING, RETSUKO.
MORNING, FENNEKO.
DID YOU SEE WHAT TSUNODA POSTED LAST NIGHT?

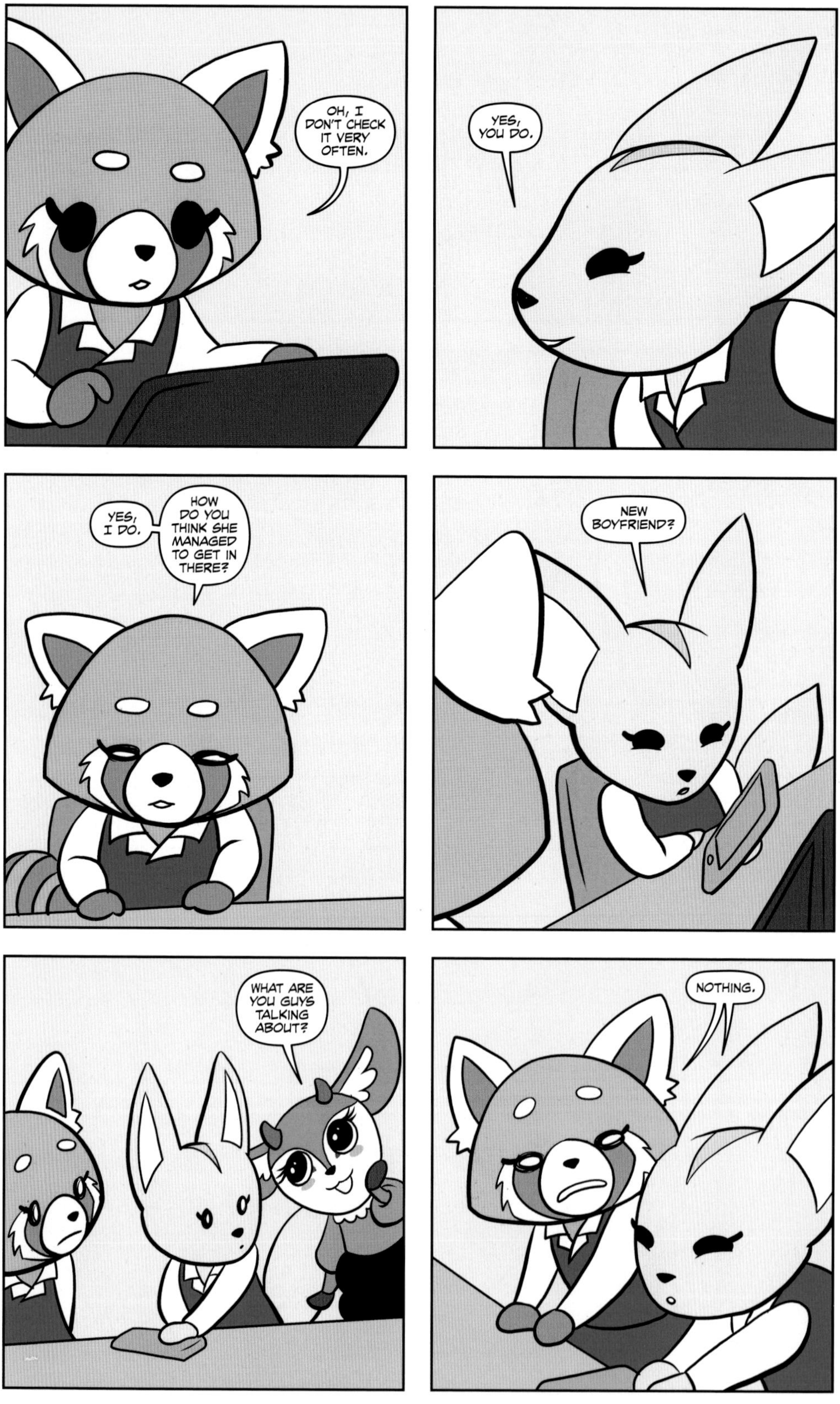

OH, I DON'T CHECK IT VERY OFTEN.
YES, YOU DO.
YES, I DO.
HOW DO YOU THINK SHE MANAGED TO GET IN THERE?
NEW BOYFRIEND?
WHAT ARE YOU GUYS TALKING ABOUT?
NOTHING.

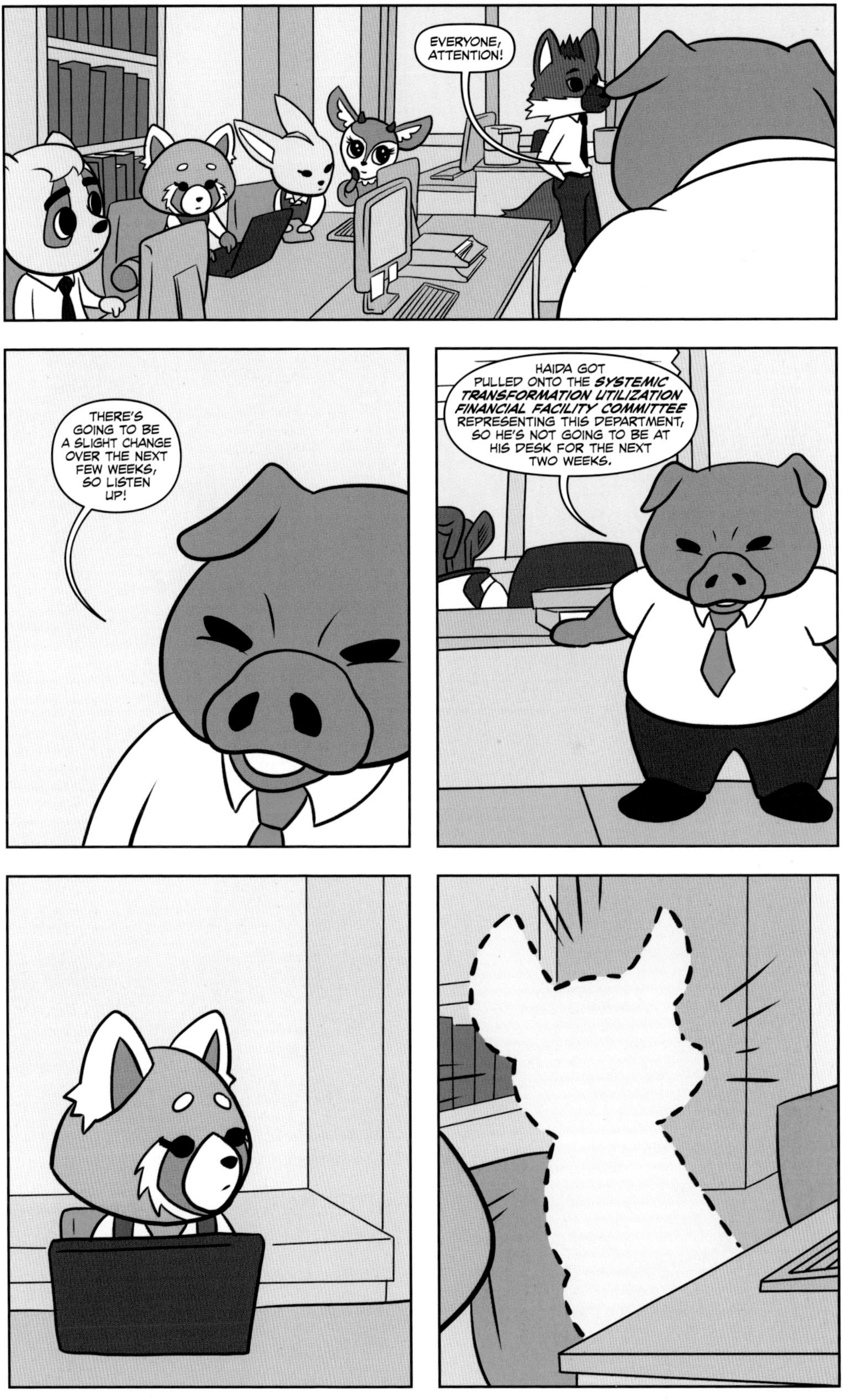
EVERYONE, ATTENTION!
THERE'S GOING TO BE A SLIGHT CHANGE OVER THE NEXT FEW WEEKS, SO LISTEN UP!
HAIDA GOT PULLED ONTO THE ***SYSTEMIC TRANSFORMATION UTILIZATION FINANCIAL FACILITY COMMITTEE*** REPRESENTING THIS DEPARTMENT, SO HE'S NOT GOING TO BE AT HIS DESK FOR THE NEXT TWO WEEKS.

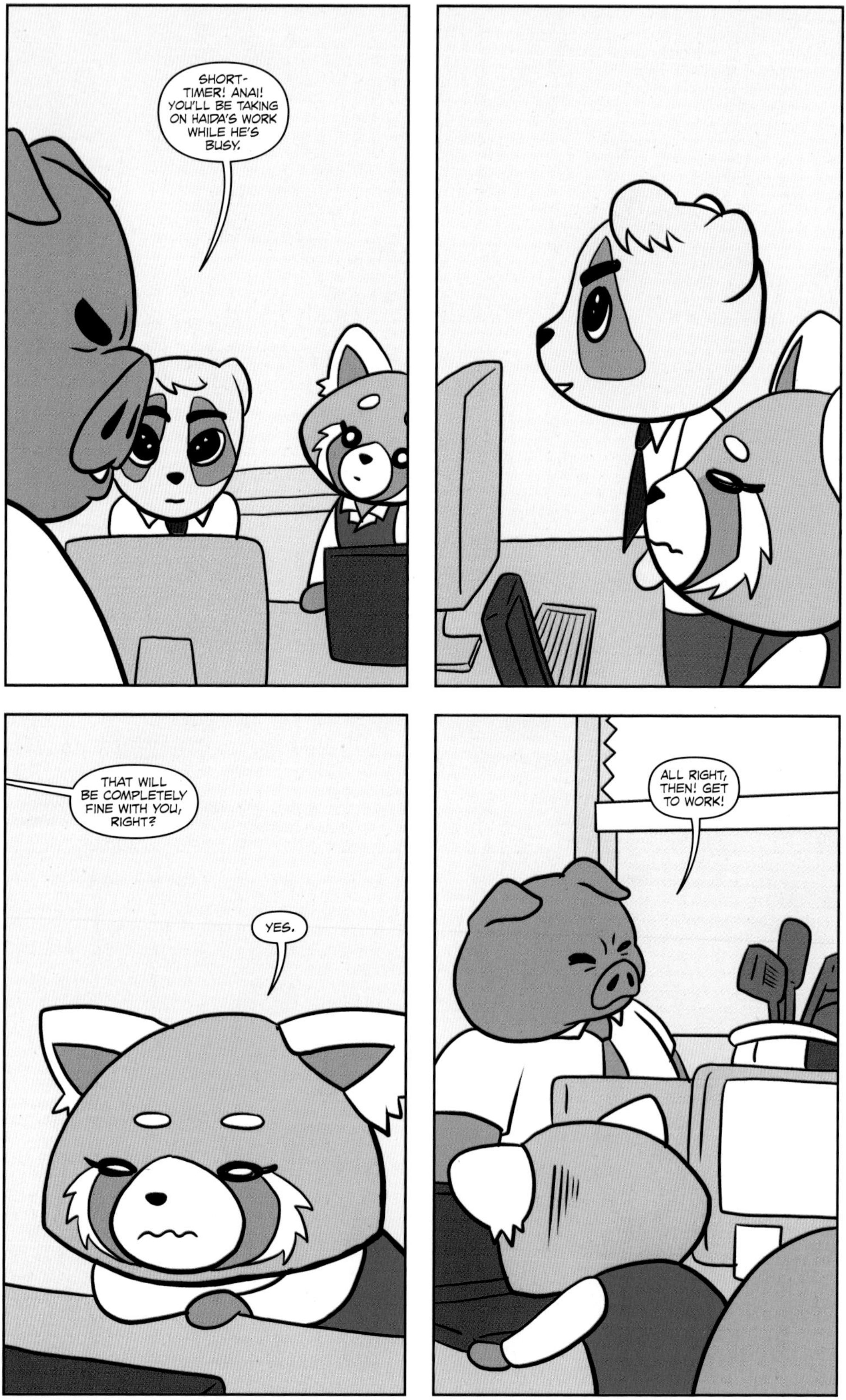
SHORT-TIMER! ANAI! YOU'LL BE TAKING ON HAIDA'S WORK WHILE HE'S BUSY.
THAT WILL BE COMPLETELY FINE WITH YOU, RIGHT?
YES.
ALL RIGHT, THEN! GET TO WORK!

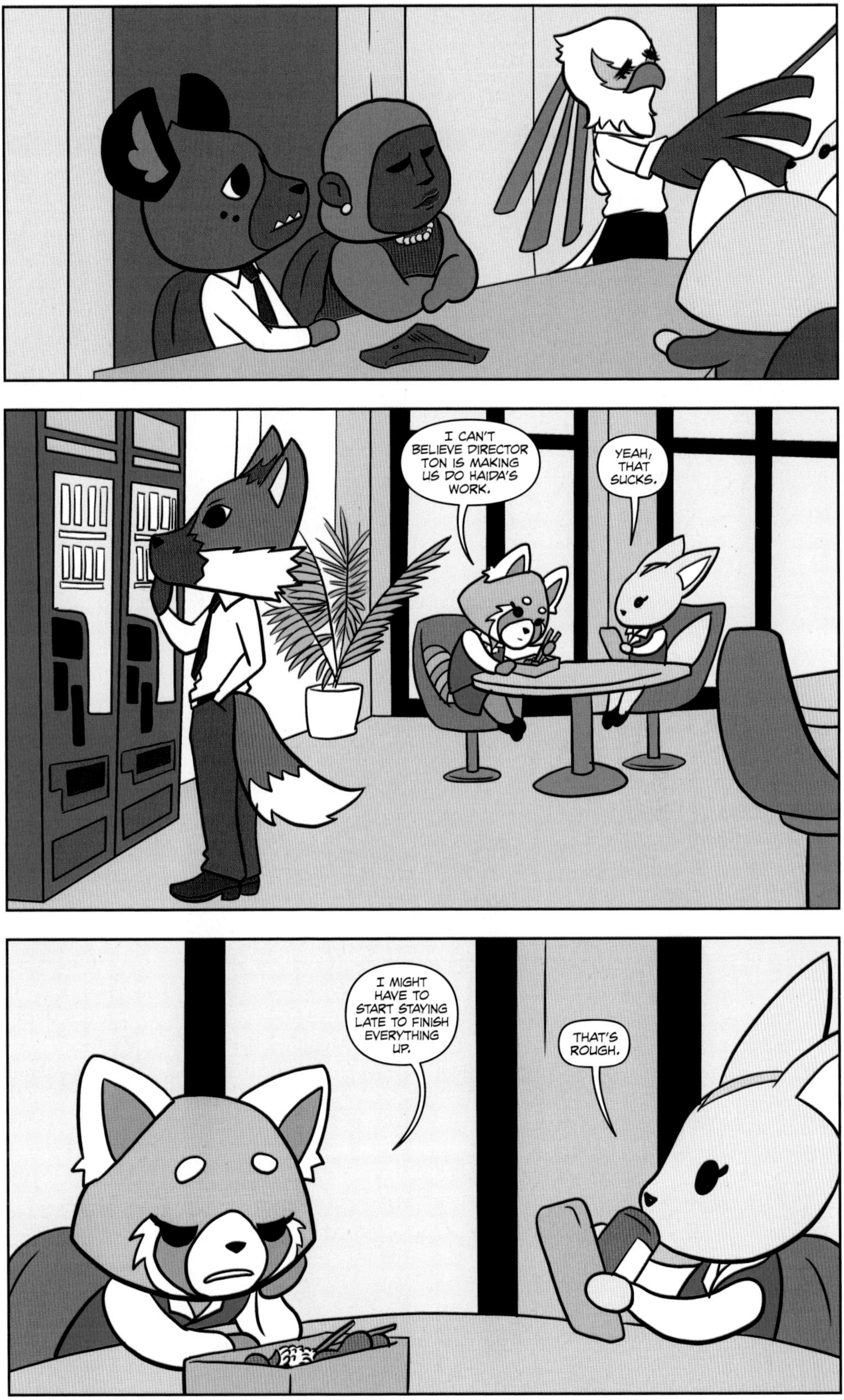
I CAN'T BELIEVE DIRECTOR TON IS MAKING US DO HAIDA'S WORK.
YEAH, THAT SUCKS.
I MIGHT HAVE TO START STAYING LATE TO FINISH EVERYTHING UP.
THAT'S ROUGH.

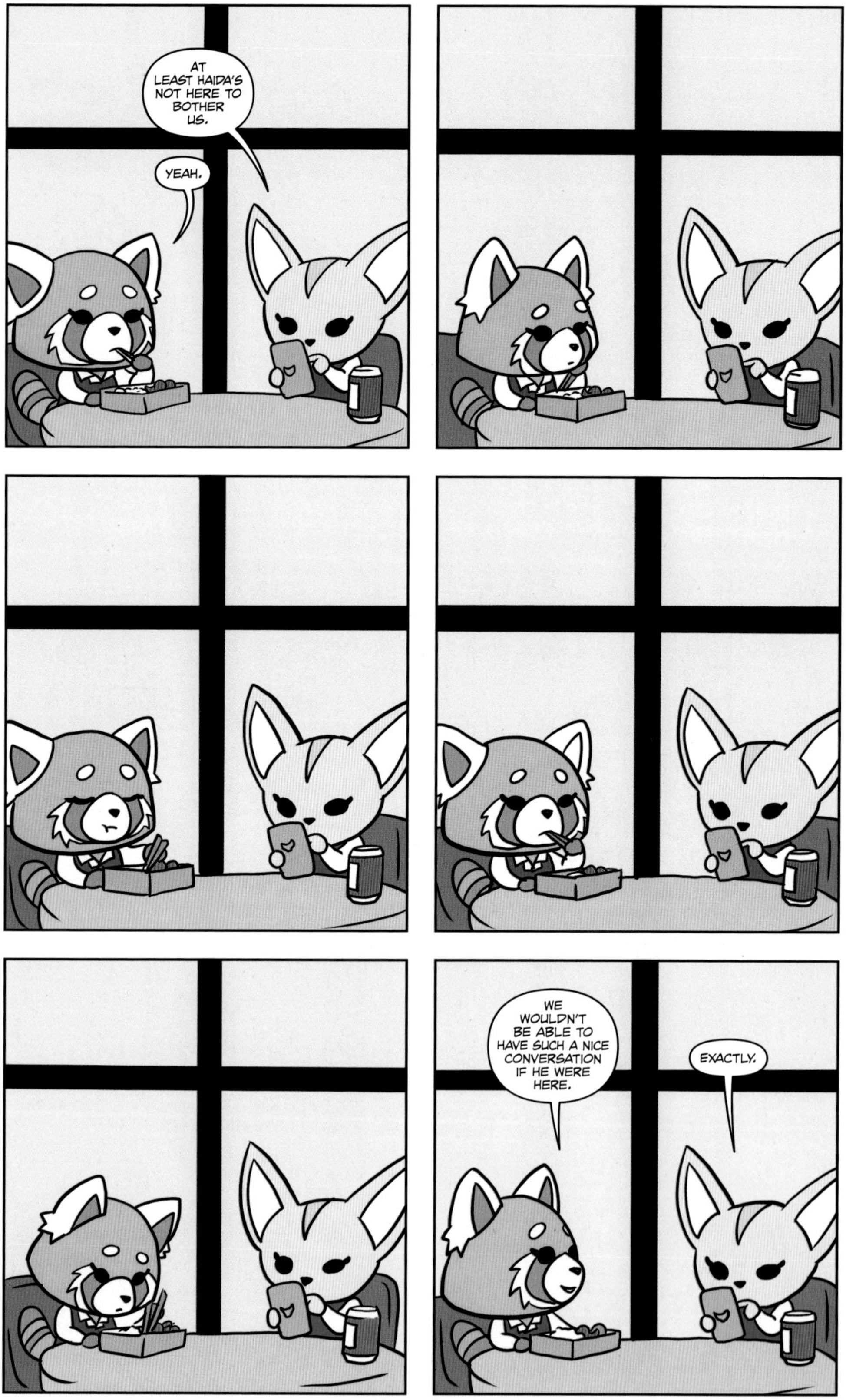
AT LEAST HAIDA'S NOT HERE TO BOTHER US.
YEAH.
WE WOULDN'T BE ABLE TO HAVE SUCH A NICE CONVERSATION IF HE WERE HERE.
EXACTLY.

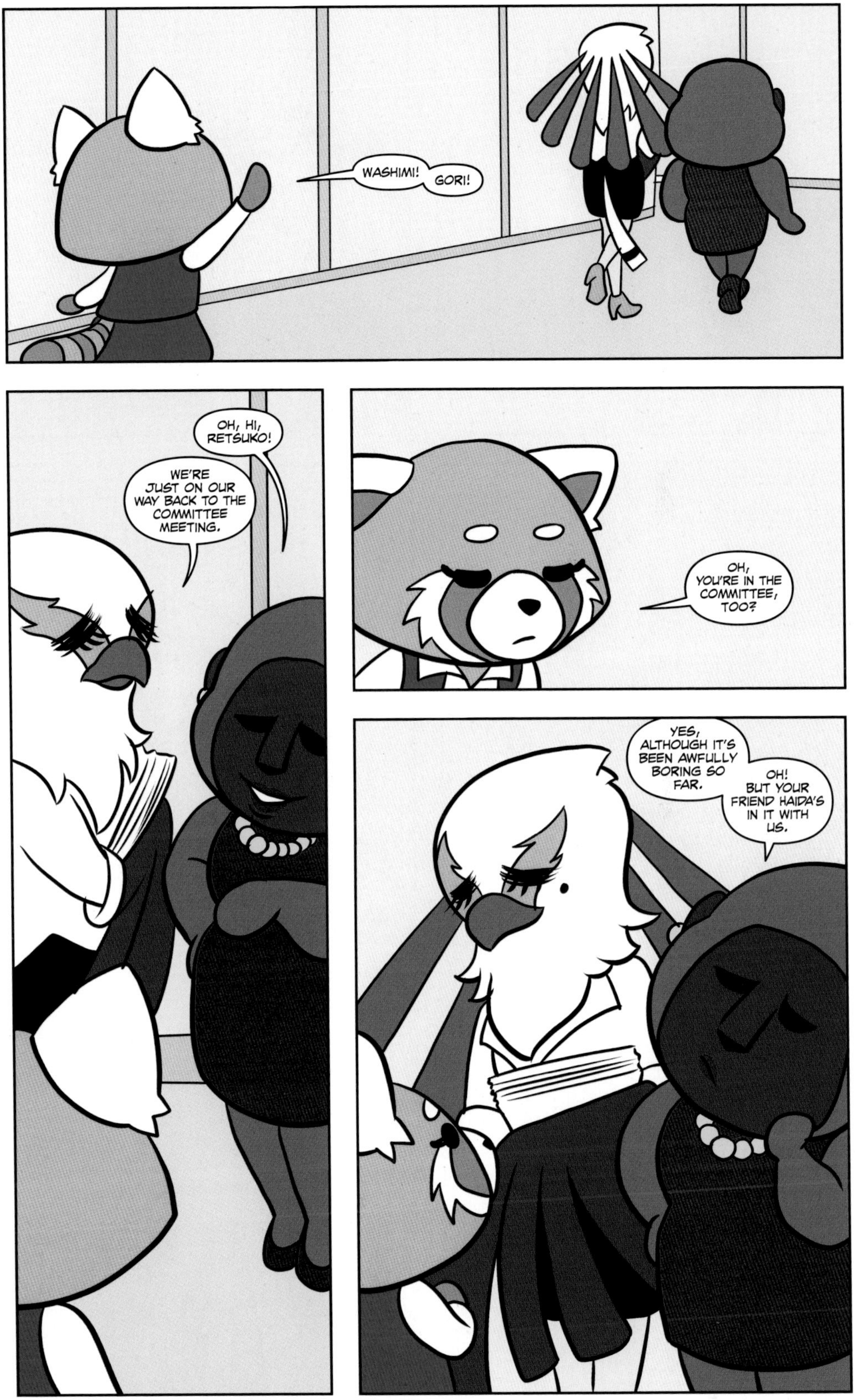
WASHIMI!
GORI!
OH, HI, RETSUKO!
WE'RE JUST ON OUR WAY BACK TO THE COMMITTEE MEETING.
OH, YOU'RE IN THE COMMITTEE, TOO?
YES, ALTHOUGH IT'S BEEN AWFULLY BORING SO FAR.
OH! BUT YOUR FRIEND HAIDA'S IN IT WITH US.

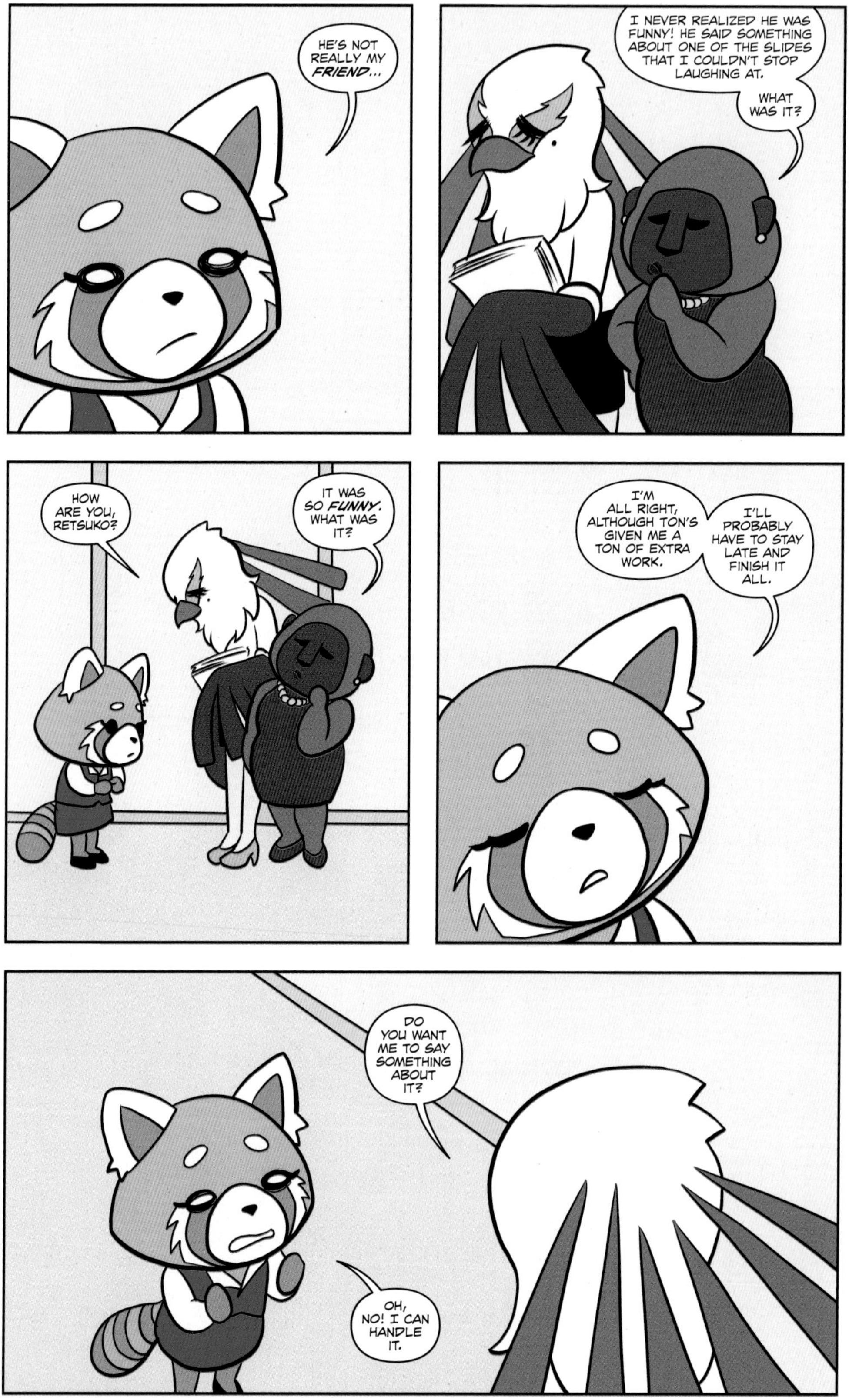
HE'S NOT REALLY MY *FRIEND*...
I NEVER REALIZED HE WAS FUNNY! HE SAID SOMETHING ABOUT ONE OF THE SLIDES THAT I COULDN'T STOP LAUGHING AT.
WHAT WAS IT?
HOW ARE YOU, RETSUKO?
IT WAS SO *FUNNY*. WHAT WAS IT?
I'M ALL RIGHT, ALTHOUGH TON'S GIVEN ME A TON OF EXTRA WORK.
I'LL PROBABLY HAVE TO STAY LATE AND FINISH IT ALL.
DO YOU WANT ME TO SAY SOMETHING ABOUT IT?
OH, NO! I CAN HANDLE IT.

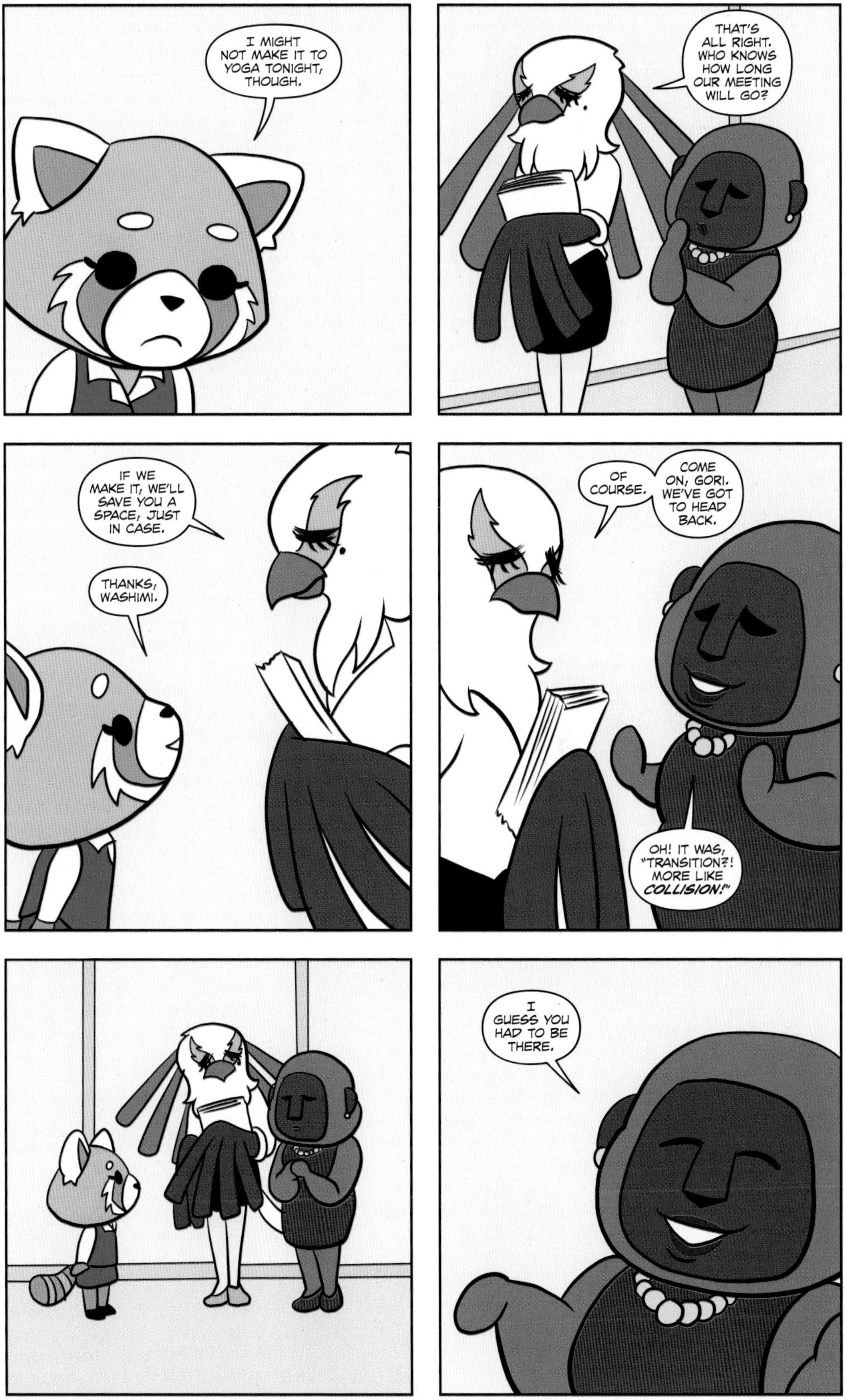
I MIGHT NOT MAKE IT TO YOGA TONIGHT, THOUGH.
THAT'S ALL RIGHT. WHO KNOWS HOW LONG OUR MEETING WILL GO?
IF WE MAKE IT, WE'LL SAVE YOU A SPACE, JUST IN CASE.
THANKS, WASHIMI.
COME ON, GORI. WE'VE GOT TO HEAD BACK.
OF COURSE.
OH! IT WAS, "TRANSITION?! MORE LIKE COLLISION!"
I GUESS YOU HAD TO BE THERE.

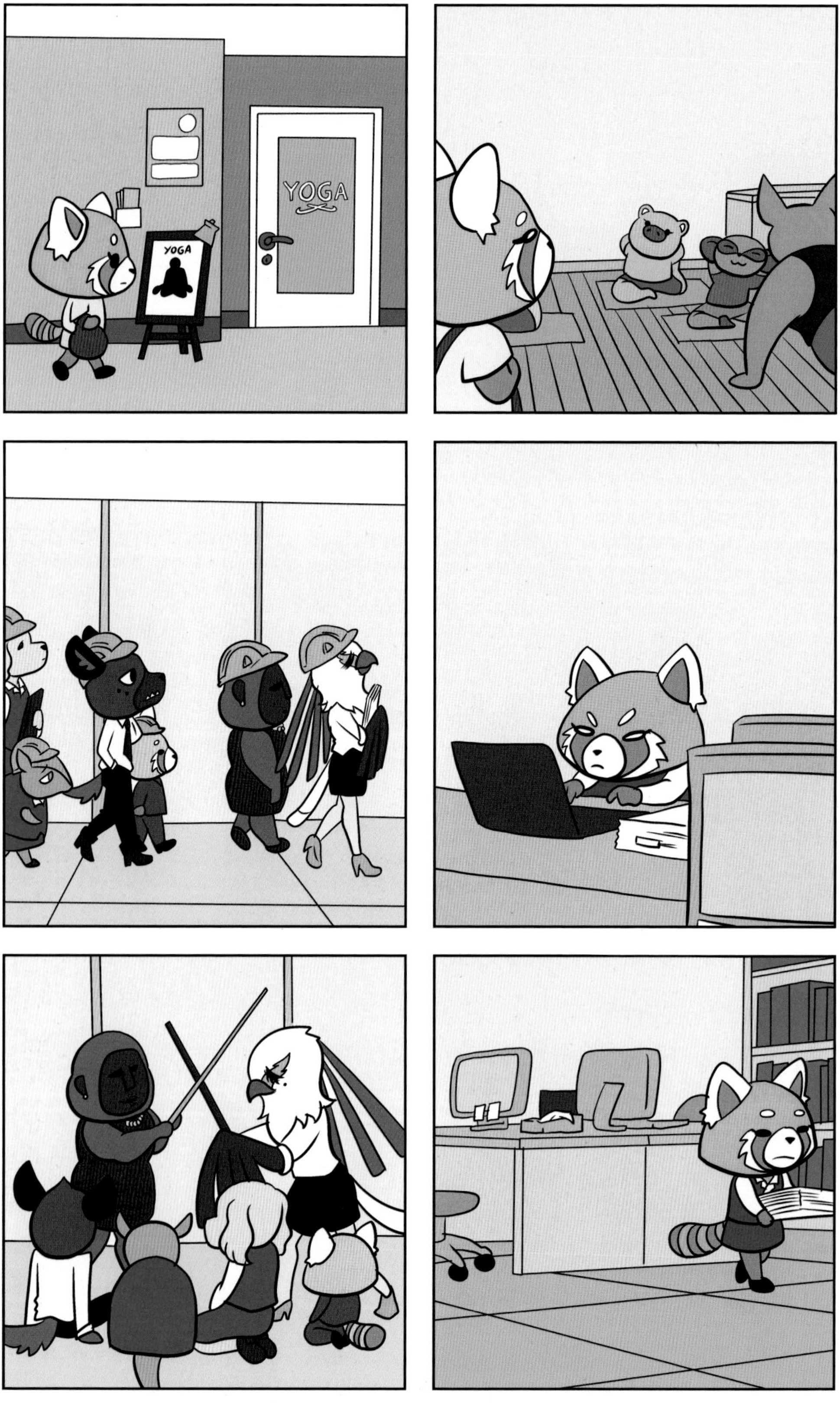
YOGA
YOGA

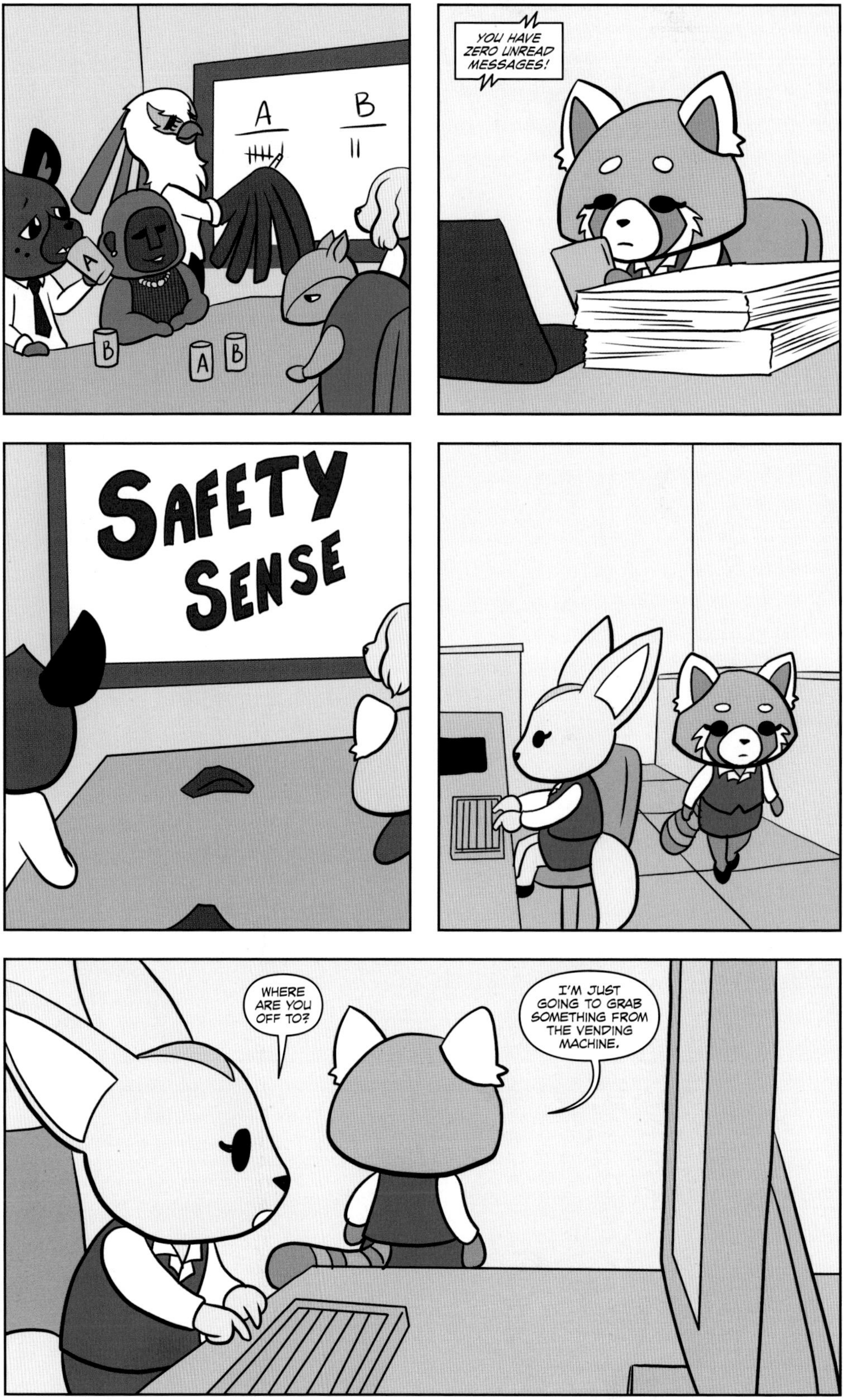
A
B
YOU HAVE ZERO UNREAD MESSAGES!
SAFETY SENSE
WHERE ARE YOU OFF TO?
I'M JUST GOING TO GRAB SOMETHING FROM THE VENDING MACHINE.

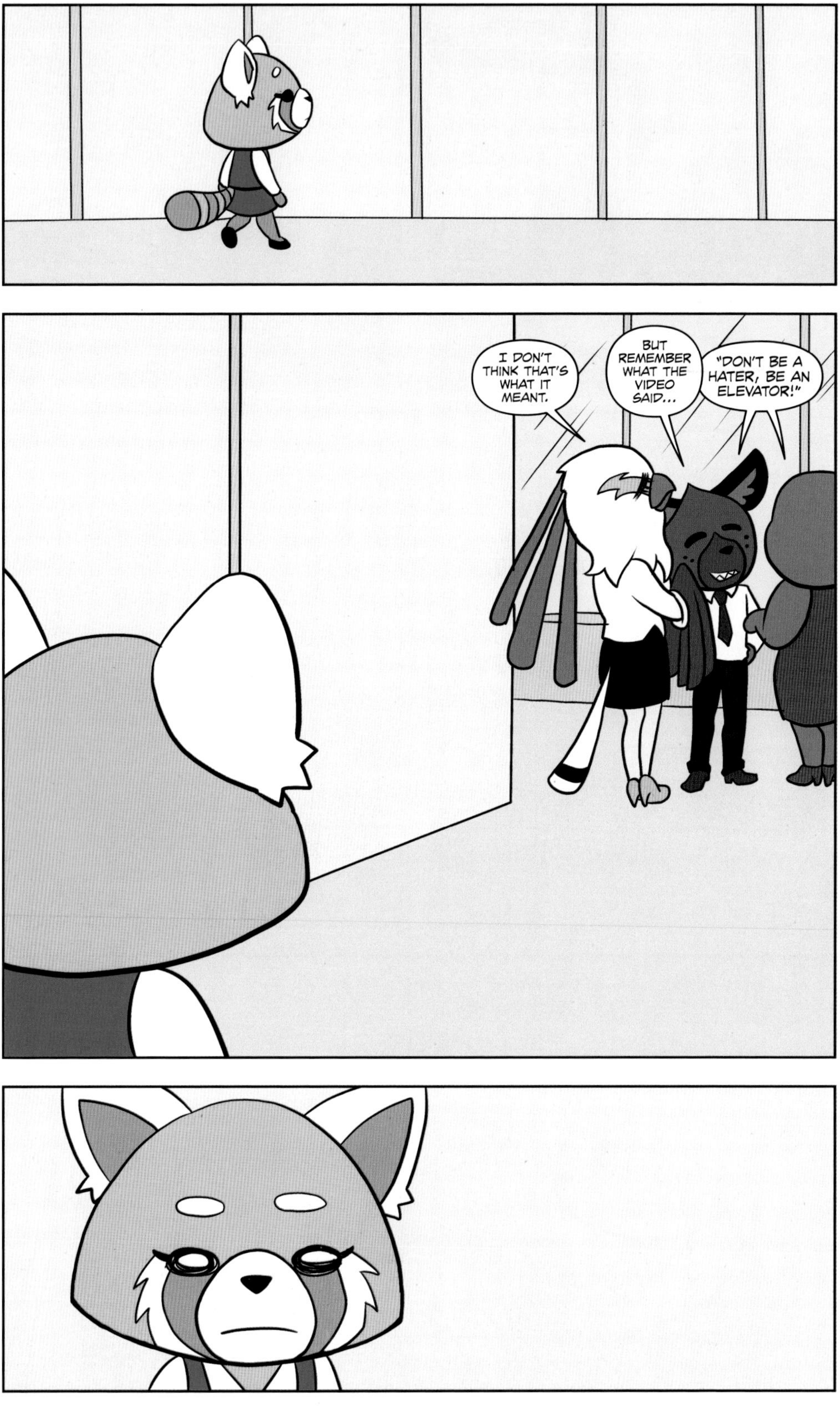
I DON'T THINK THAT'S WHAT IT MEANT.
BUT REMEMBER WHAT THE VIDEO SAID...
"DON'T BE A HATER, BE AN ELEVATOR!"

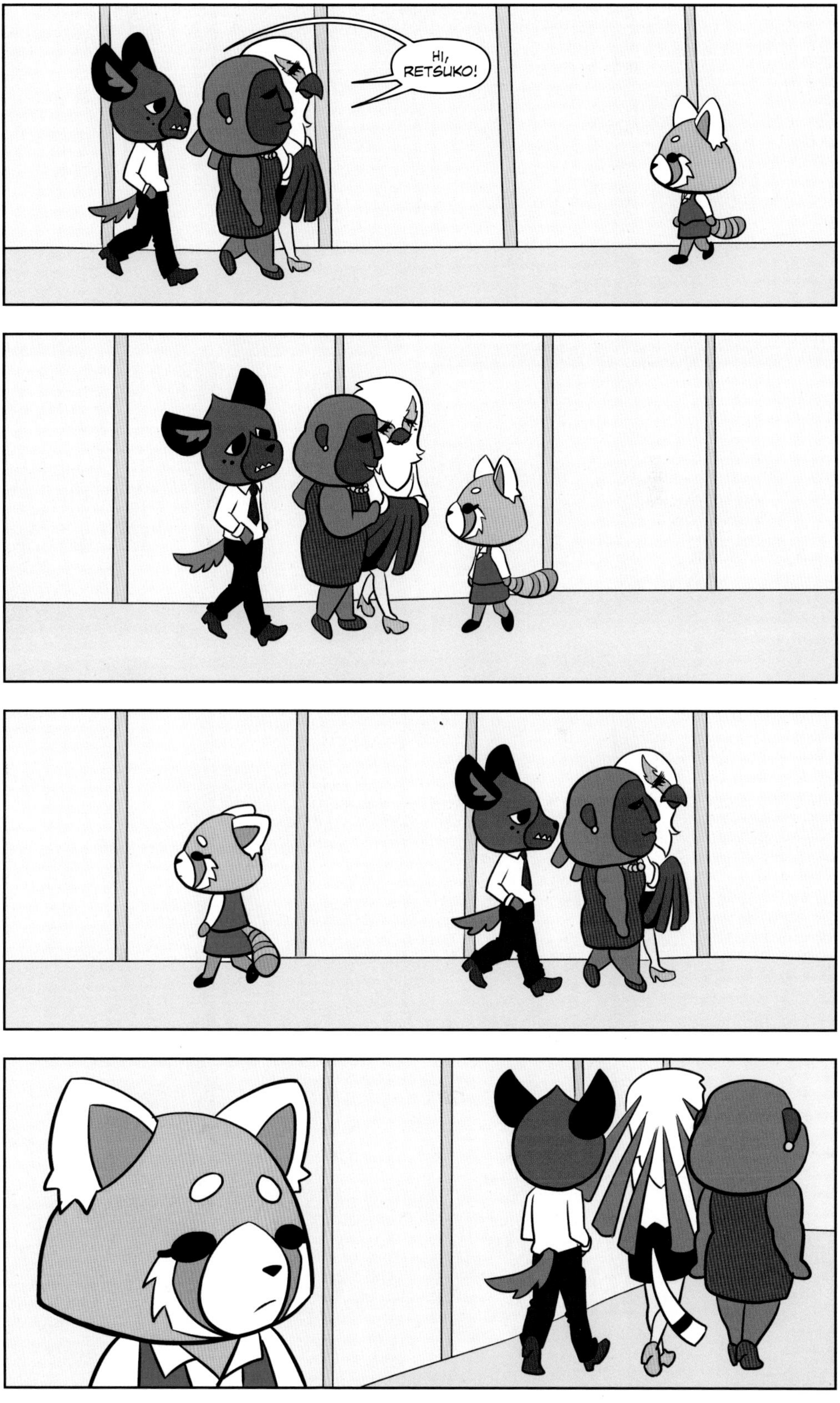
HI, RETSUKO!

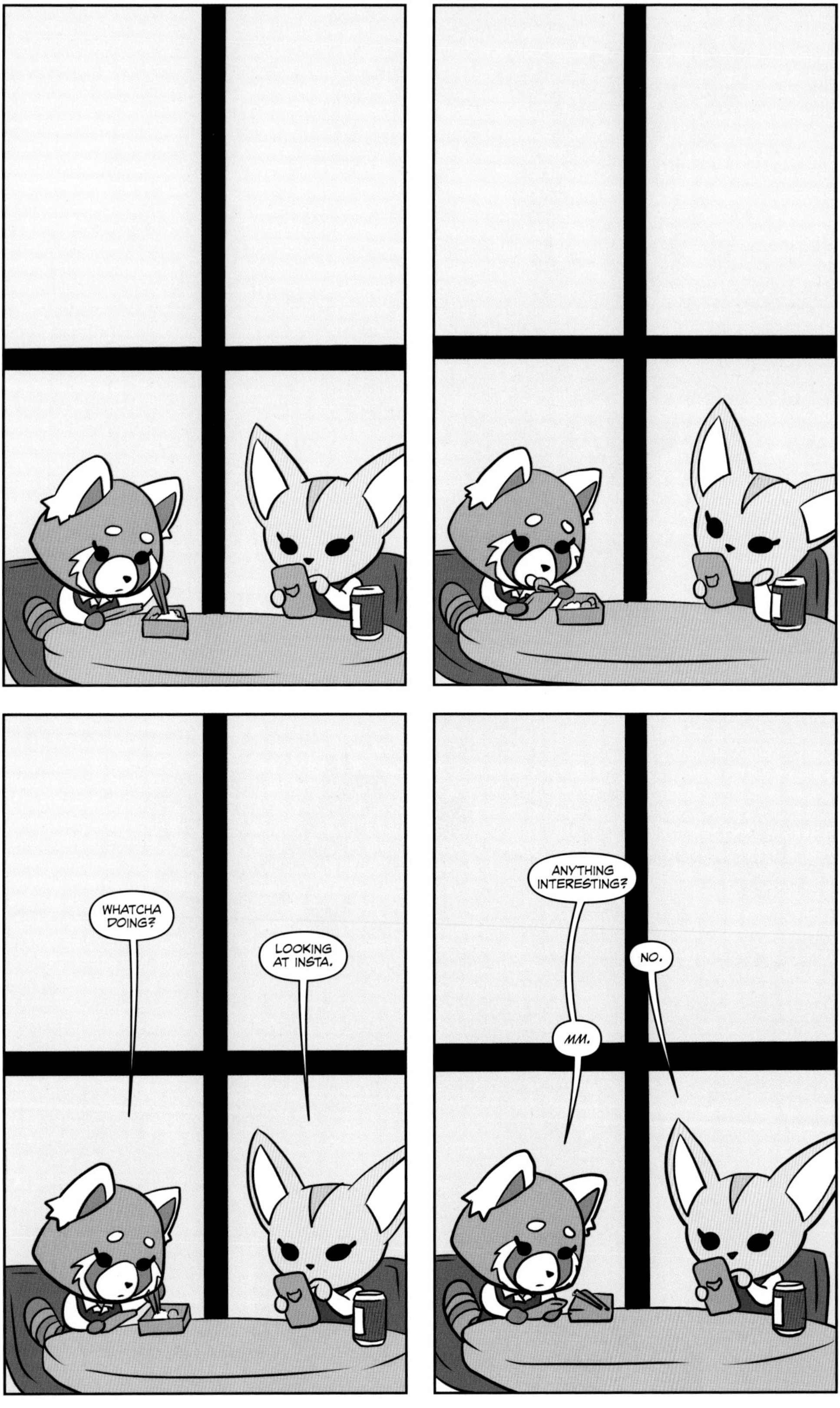
WHATCHA DOING?
LOOKING AT INSTA.
ANYTHING INTERESTING?
NO.
MM.

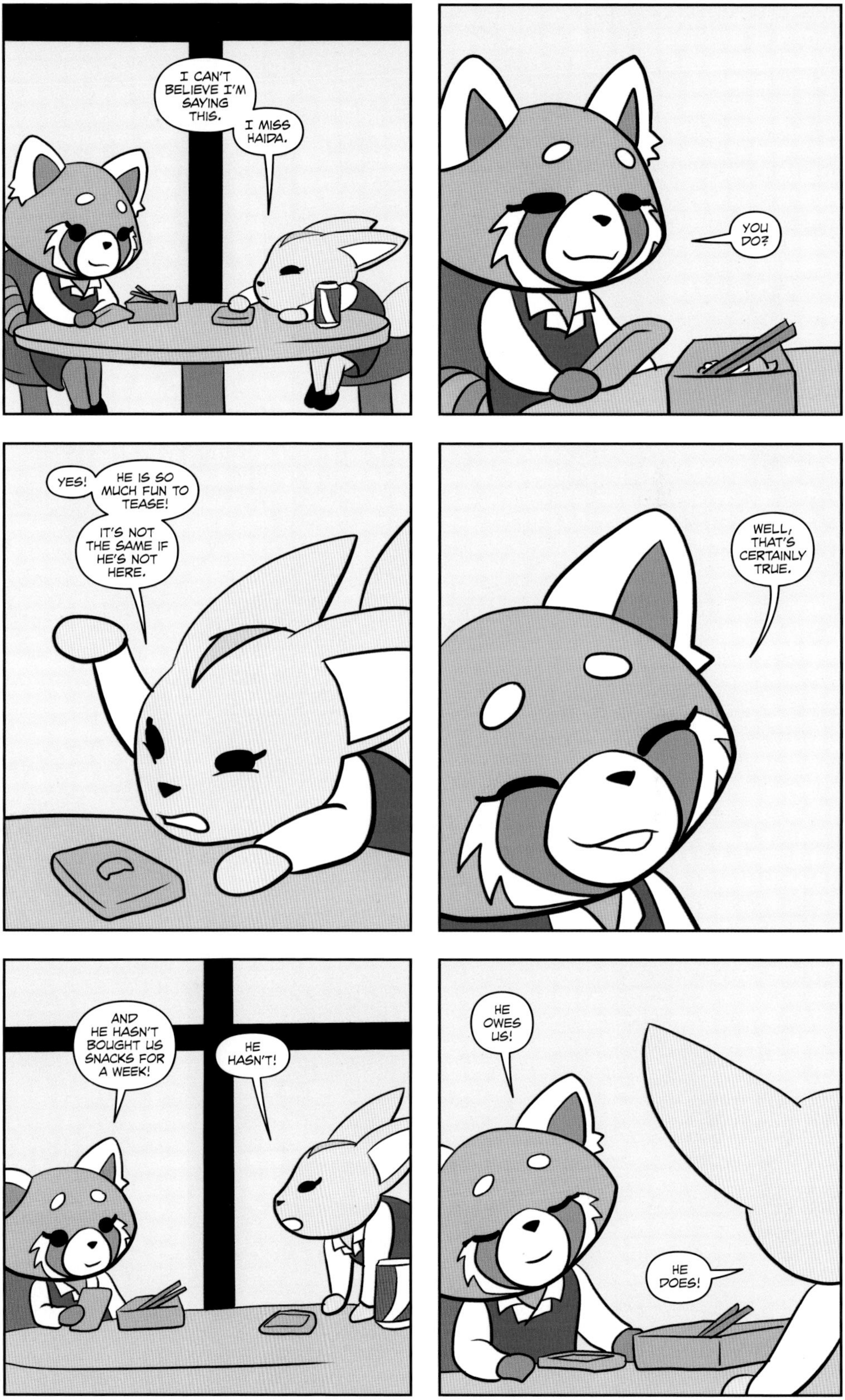
I CAN'T BELIEVE I'M SAYING THIS.
I MISS HAIDA.
YOU DO?
YES!
HE IS SO MUCH FUN TO TEASE!
IT'S NOT THE SAME IF HE'S NOT HERE.
WELL, THAT'S CERTAINLY TRUE.
AND HE HASN'T BOUGHT US SNACKS FOR A WEEK!
HE HASN'T!
HE OWES US!
HE DOES!

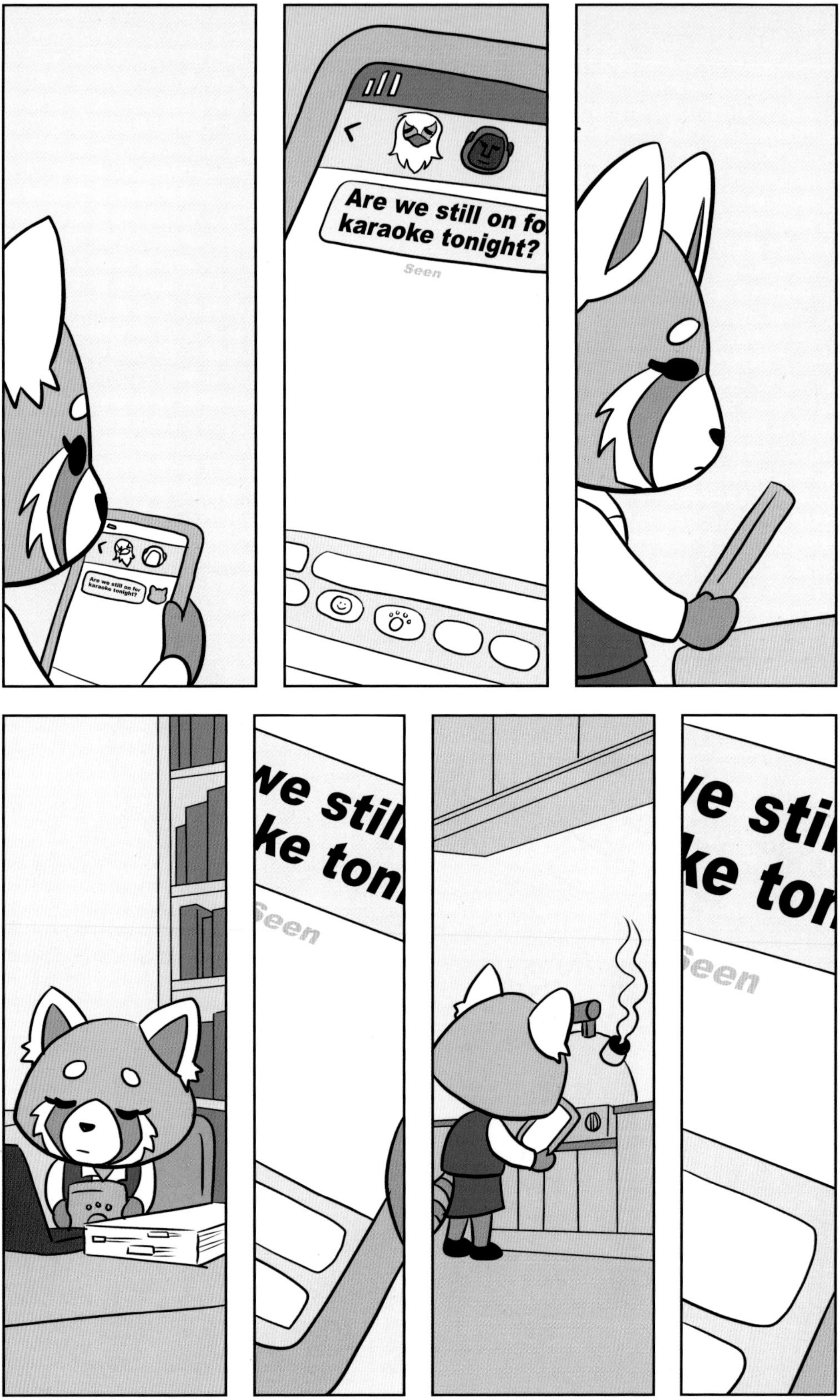
Are we still on for karaoke tonight?
Are we still on fo
karaoke tonight?
Seen
we stil
ke ton
Seen
we sti
ke ton
Seen

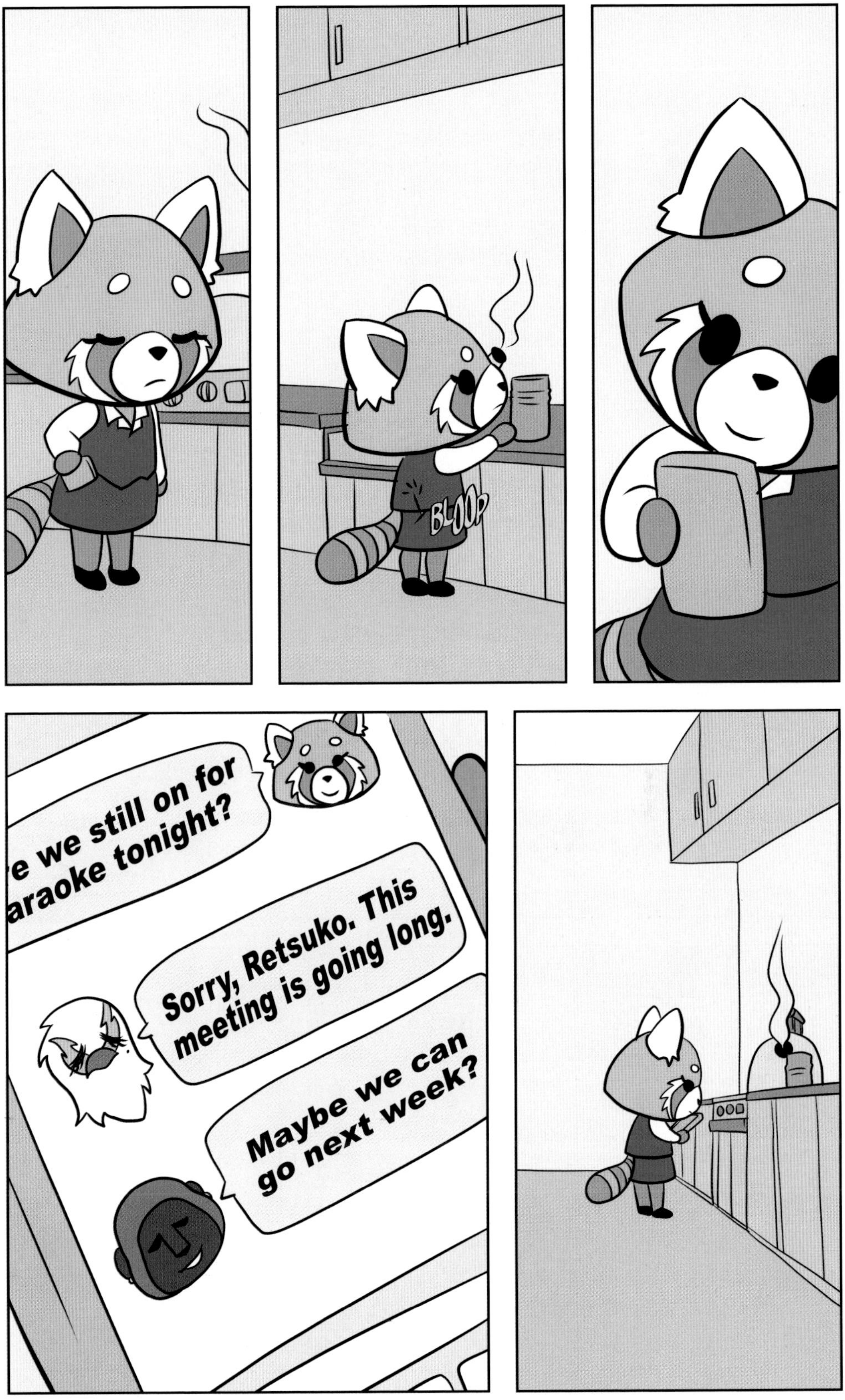
BLOOP
e we still on for araoke tonight?
Sorry, Retsuko. This meeting is going long.
Maybe we can go next week?

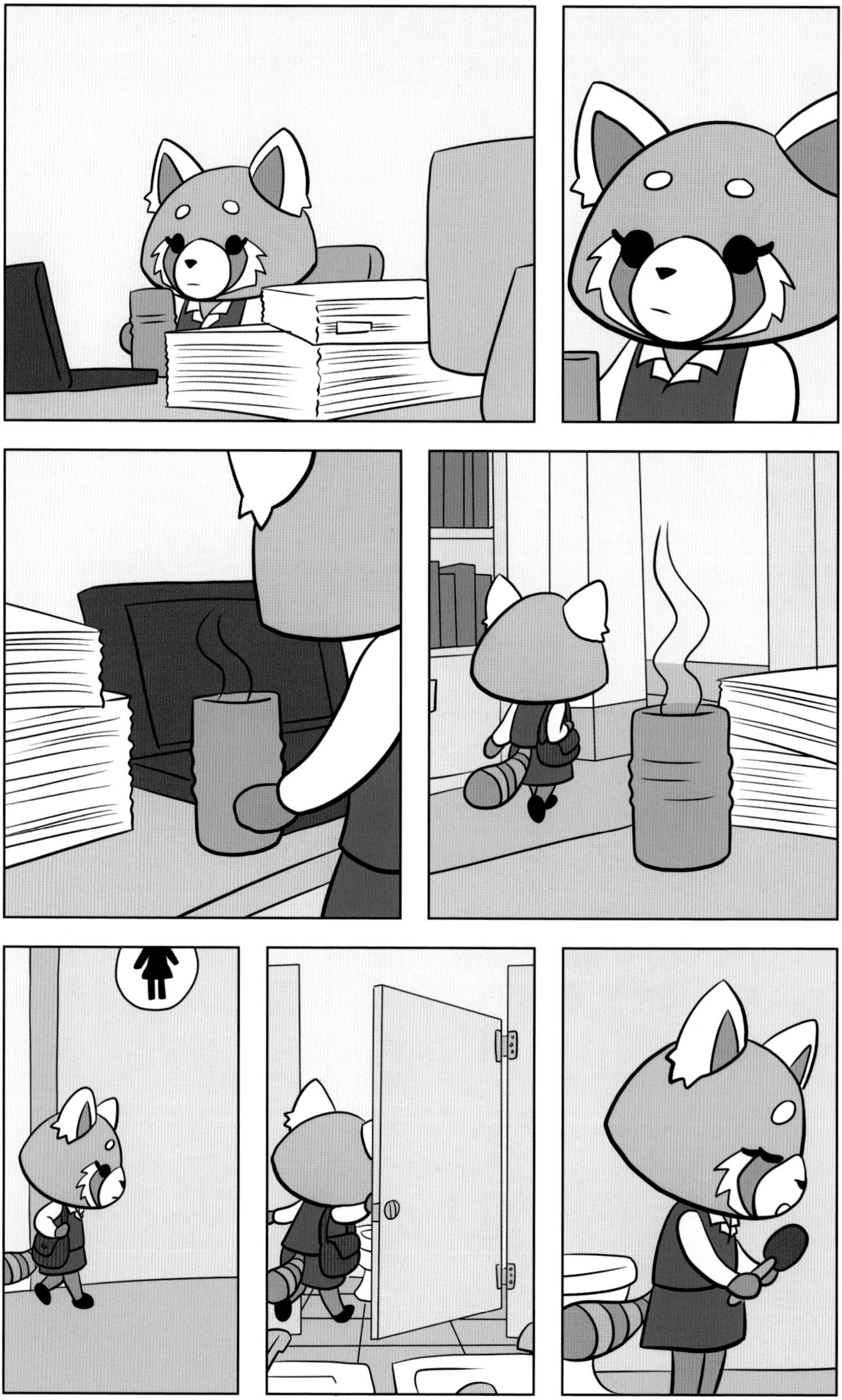

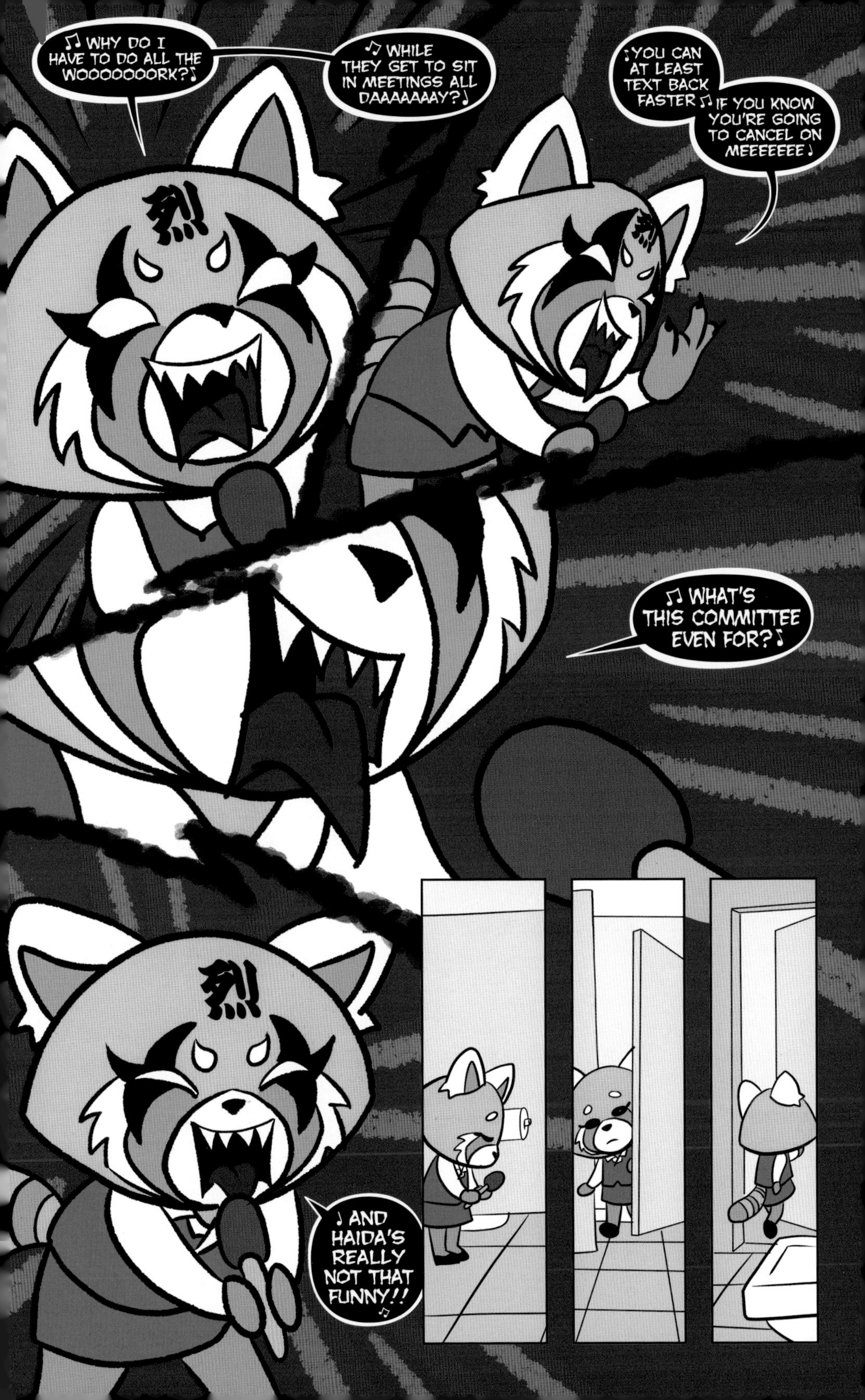
♫ WHY DO I HAVE TO DO ALL THE WOOOOOOOORK?♪
♫ WHILE THEY GET TO SIT IN MEETINGS ALL DAAAAAAAY?♪
♪YOU CAN AT LEAST TEXT BACK FASTER ♫
IF YOU KNOW YOU'RE GOING TO CANCEL ON MEEEEEEE♪
♫ WHAT'S THIS COMMITTEE EVEN FOR?♪
♪ AND HAIDA'S REALLY NOT THAT FUNNY!! ♫

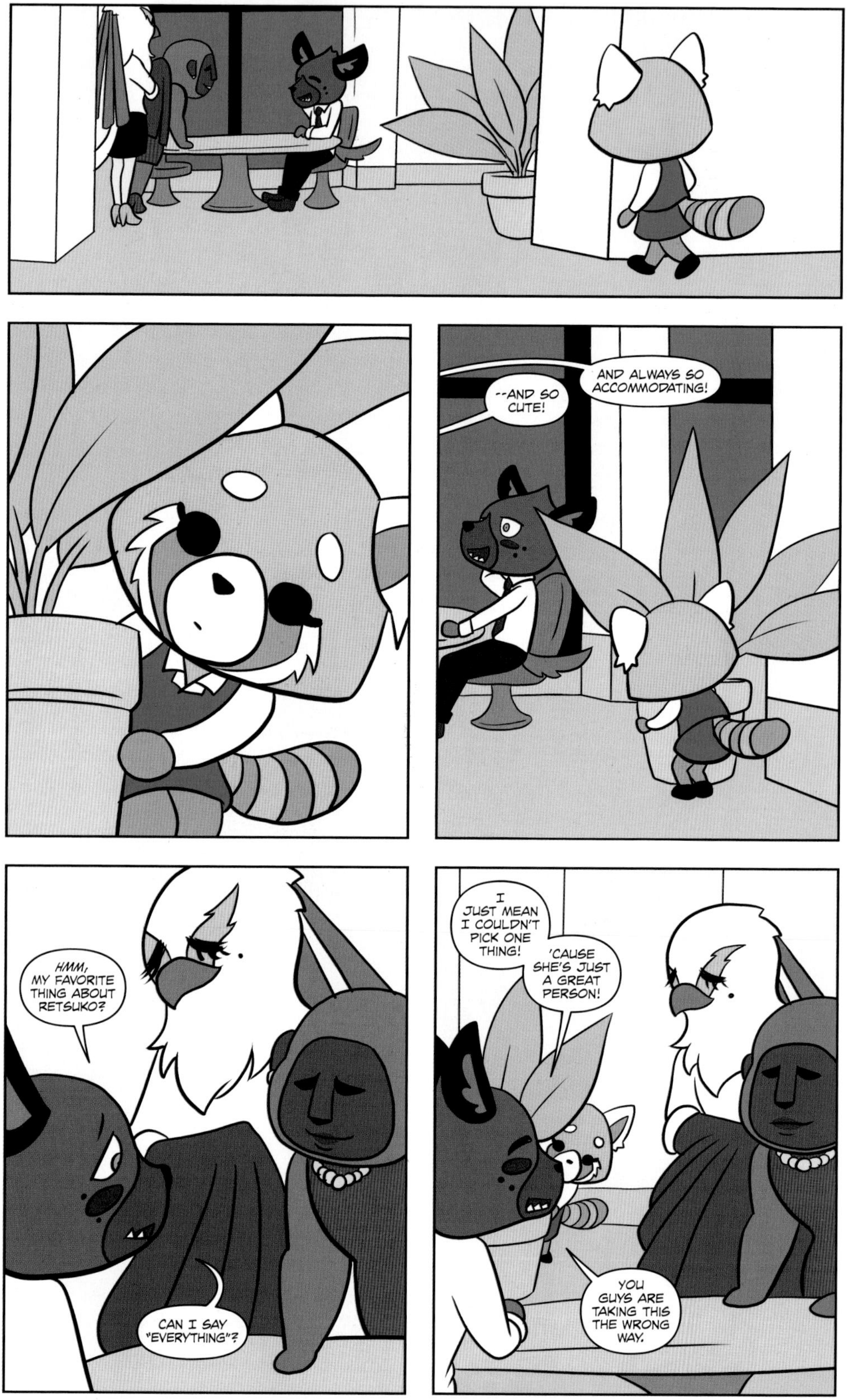
--AND SO CUTE!
AND ALWAYS SO ACCOMMODATING!
HMM, MY FAVORITE THING ABOUT RETSUKO?
CAN I SAY "EVERYTHING"?
I JUST MEAN I COULDN'T PICK ONE THING!
'CAUSE SHE'S JUST A GREAT PERSON!
YOU GUYS ARE TAKING THIS THE WRONG WAY.

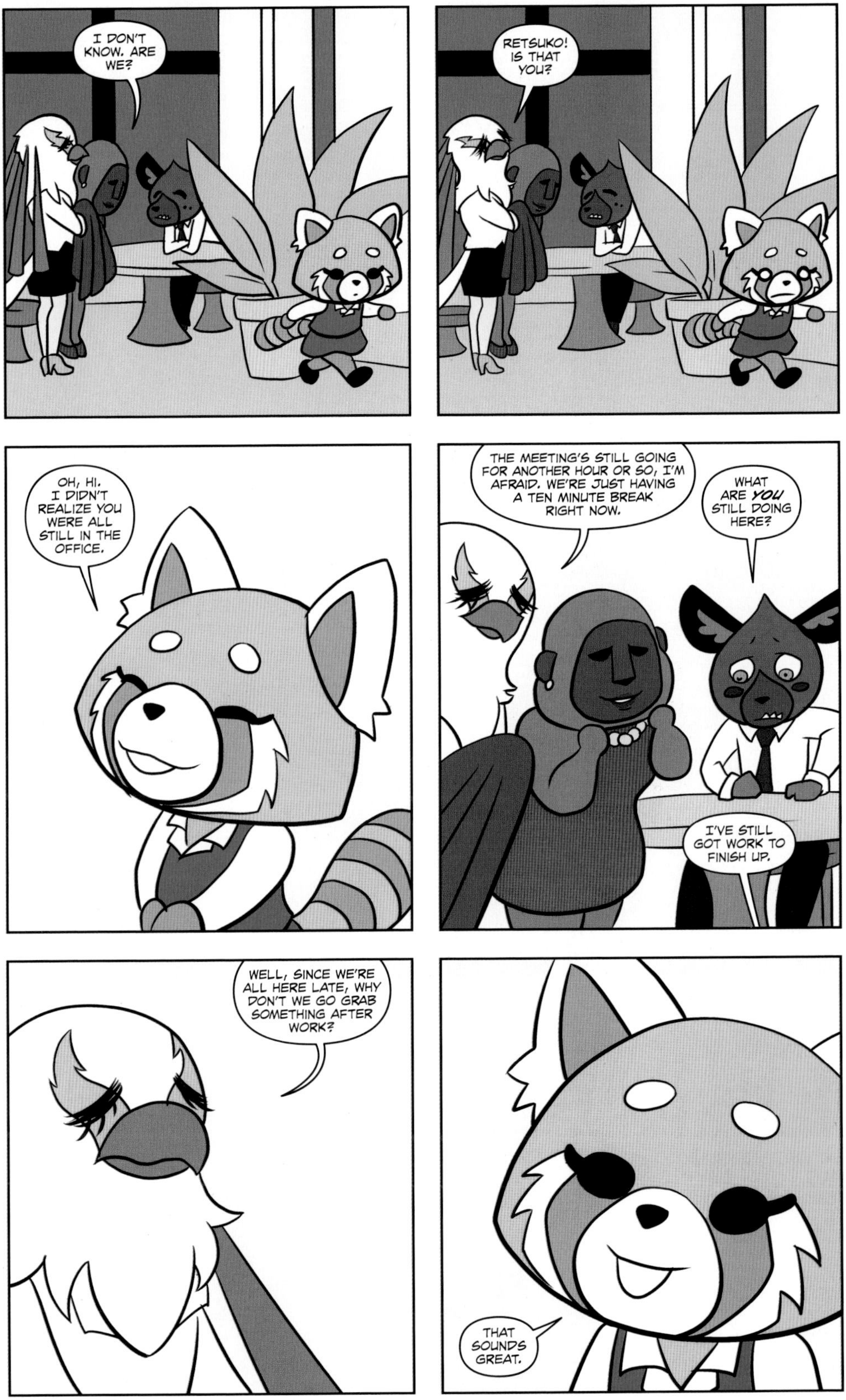
I DON'T KNOW. ARE WE?
RETSUKO! IS THAT YOU?
OH, HI. I DIDN'T REALIZE YOU WERE ALL STILL IN THE OFFICE.
THE MEETING'S STILL GOING FOR ANOTHER HOUR OR SO, I'M AFRAID. WE'RE JUST HAVING A TEN MINUTE BREAK RIGHT NOW.
WHAT ARE YOU STILL DOING HERE?
I'VE STILL GOT WORK TO FINISH UP.
WELL, SINCE WE'RE ALL HERE LATE, WHY DON'T WE GO GRAB SOMETHING AFTER WORK?
THAT SOUNDS GREAT.

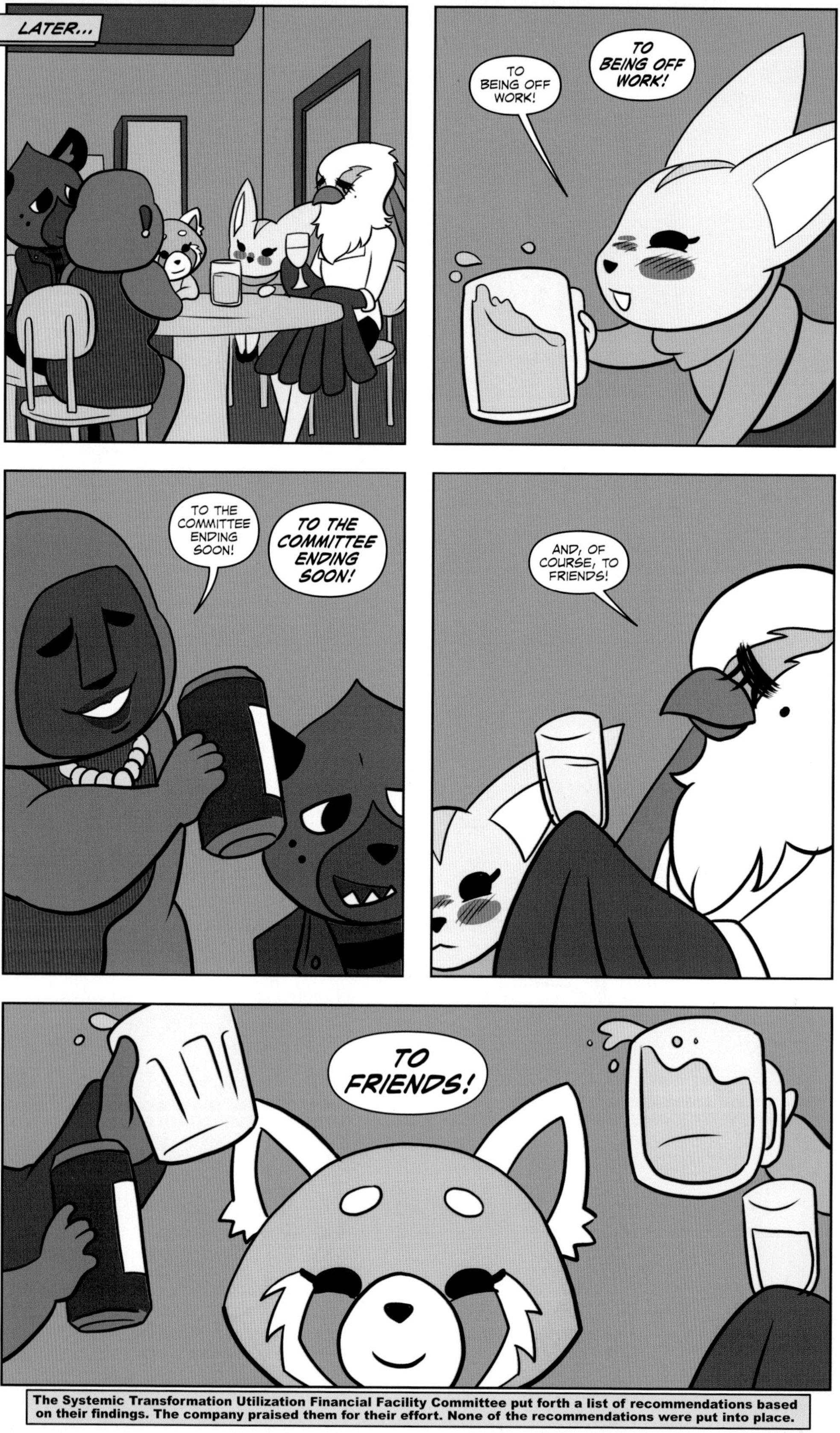
LATER...
TO BEING OFF WORK!
TO BEING OFF WORK!
TO THE COMMITTEE ENDING SOON!
TO THE COMMITTEE ENDING SOON!
AND, OF COURSE, TO FRIENDS!
TO FRIENDS!
The Systemic Transformation Utilization Financial Facility Committee put forth a list of recommendations based on their findings. The company praised them for their effort. None of the recommendations were put into place.

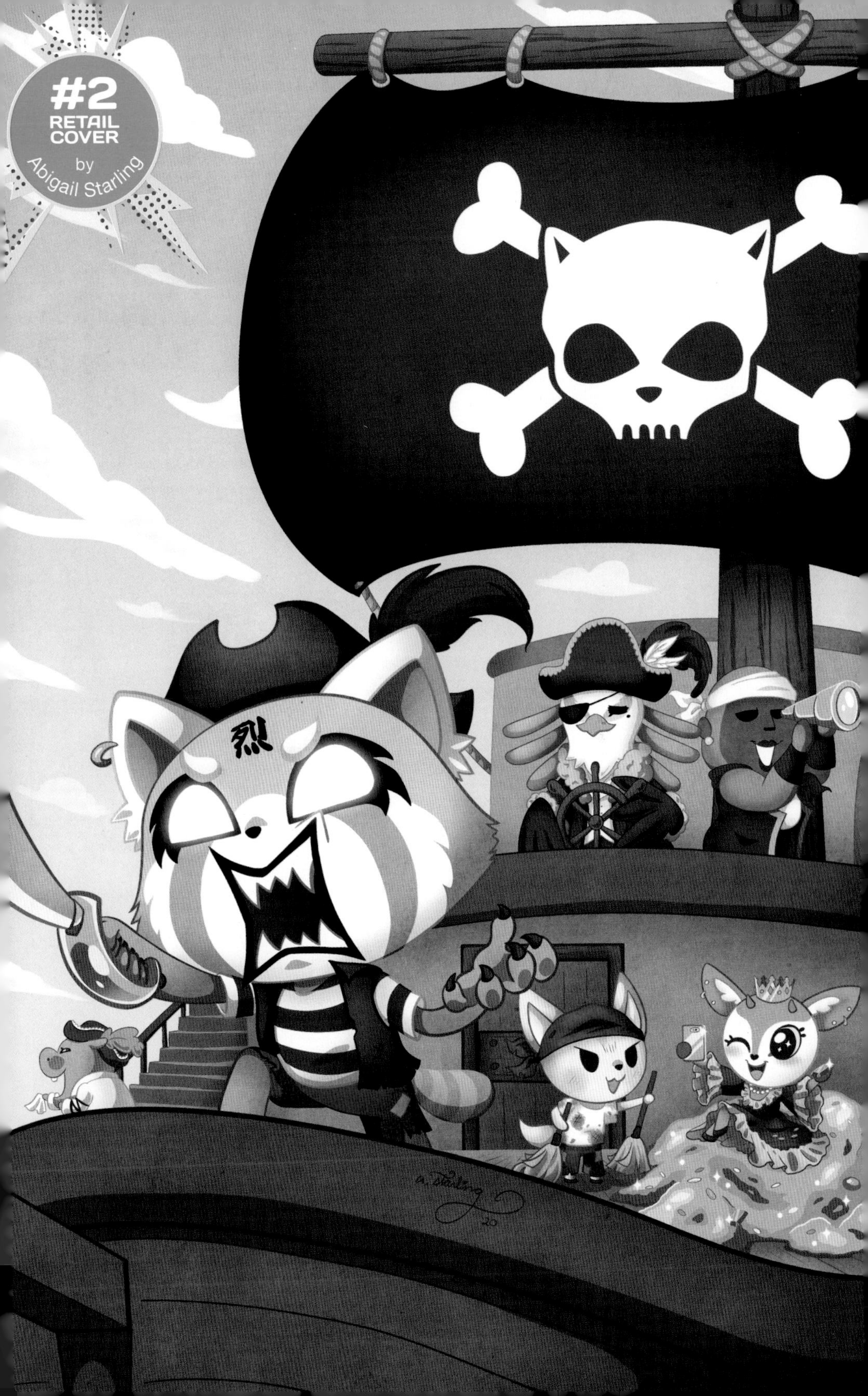
#2
RETAIL COVER
by
Abigail Starling
烈

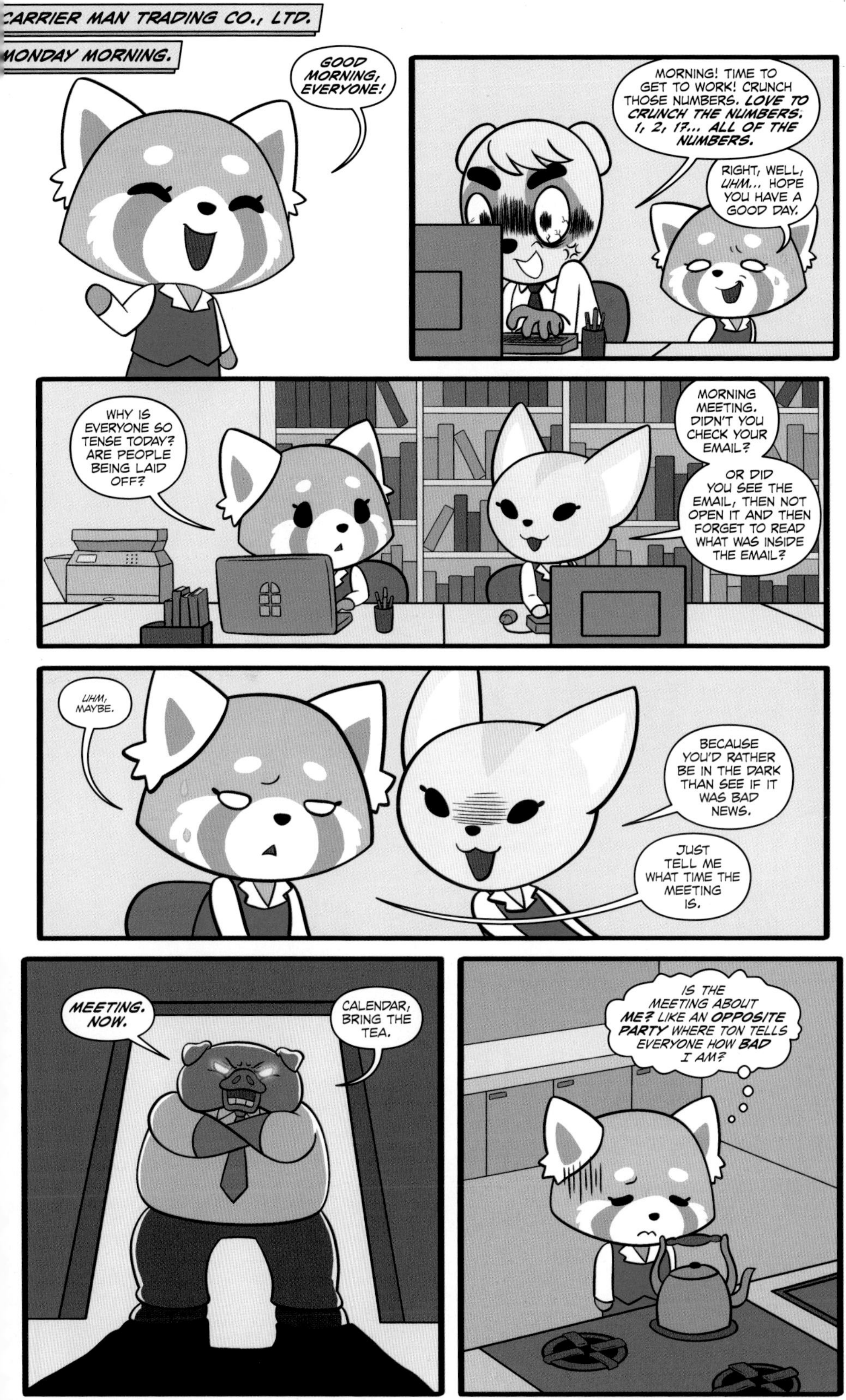
CARRIER MAN TRADING CO., LTD.
MONDAY MORNING.
GOOD MORNING, EVERYONE!
MORNING! TIME TO GET TO WORK! CRUNCH THOSE NUMBERS. LOVE TO CRUNCH THE NUMBERS. 1, 2, 17... ALL OF THE NUMBERS.
RIGHT, WELL, UHM... HOPE YOU HAVE A GOOD DAY.
WHY IS EVERYONE SO TENSE TODAY? ARE PEOPLE BEING LAID OFF?
MORNING MEETING. DIDN'T YOU CHECK YOUR EMAIL?
OR DID YOU SEE THE EMAIL, THEN NOT OPEN IT AND THEN FORGET TO READ WHAT WAS INSIDE THE EMAIL?
UHM, MAYBE.
BECAUSE YOU'D RATHER BE IN THE DARK THAN SEE IF IT WAS BAD NEWS.
JUST TELL ME WHAT TIME THE MEETING IS.
MEETING. NOW.
CALENDAR, BRING THE TEA.
IS THE MEETING ABOUT ME? LIKE AN OPPOSITE PARTY WHERE TON TELLS EVERYONE HOW BAD I AM?

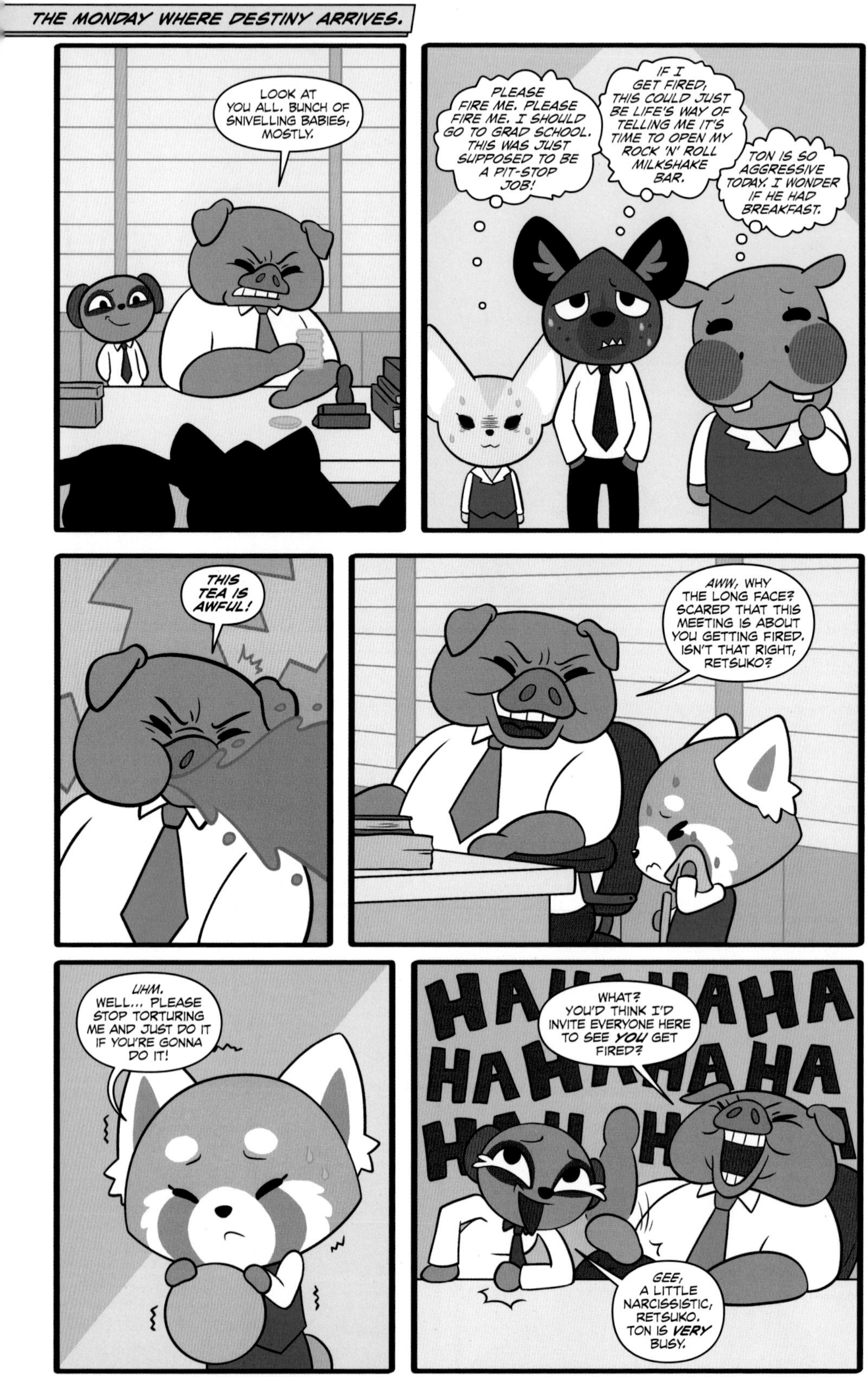
THE MONDAY WHERE DESTINY ARRIVES.
LOOK AT YOU ALL. BUNCH OF SNIVELLING BABIES, MOSTLY.
PLEASE FIRE ME. PLEASE FIRE ME. I SHOULD GO TO GRAD SCHOOL. THIS WAS JUST SUPPOSED TO BE A PIT-STOP JOB!
IF I GET FIRED, THIS COULD JUST BE LIFE'S WAY OF TELLING ME IT'S TIME TO OPEN MY ROCK 'N' ROLL MILKSHAKE BAR.
TON IS SO AGGRESSIVE TODAY. I WONDER IF HE HAD BREAKFAST.
THIS TEA IS AWFUL!
AWW, WHY THE LONG FACE? SCARED THAT THIS MEETING IS ABOUT YOU GETTING FIRED. ISN'T THAT RIGHT, RETSUKO?
UHM. WELL... PLEASE STOP TORTURING ME AND JUST DO IT IF YOU'RE GONNA DO IT!
HAHAHAHA HAHAHAHA HAHAHA
WHAT? YOU'D THINK I'D INVITE EVERYONE HERE TO SEE YOU GET FIRED?
GEE, A LITTLE NARCISSISTIC, RETSUKO. TON IS VERY BUSY.

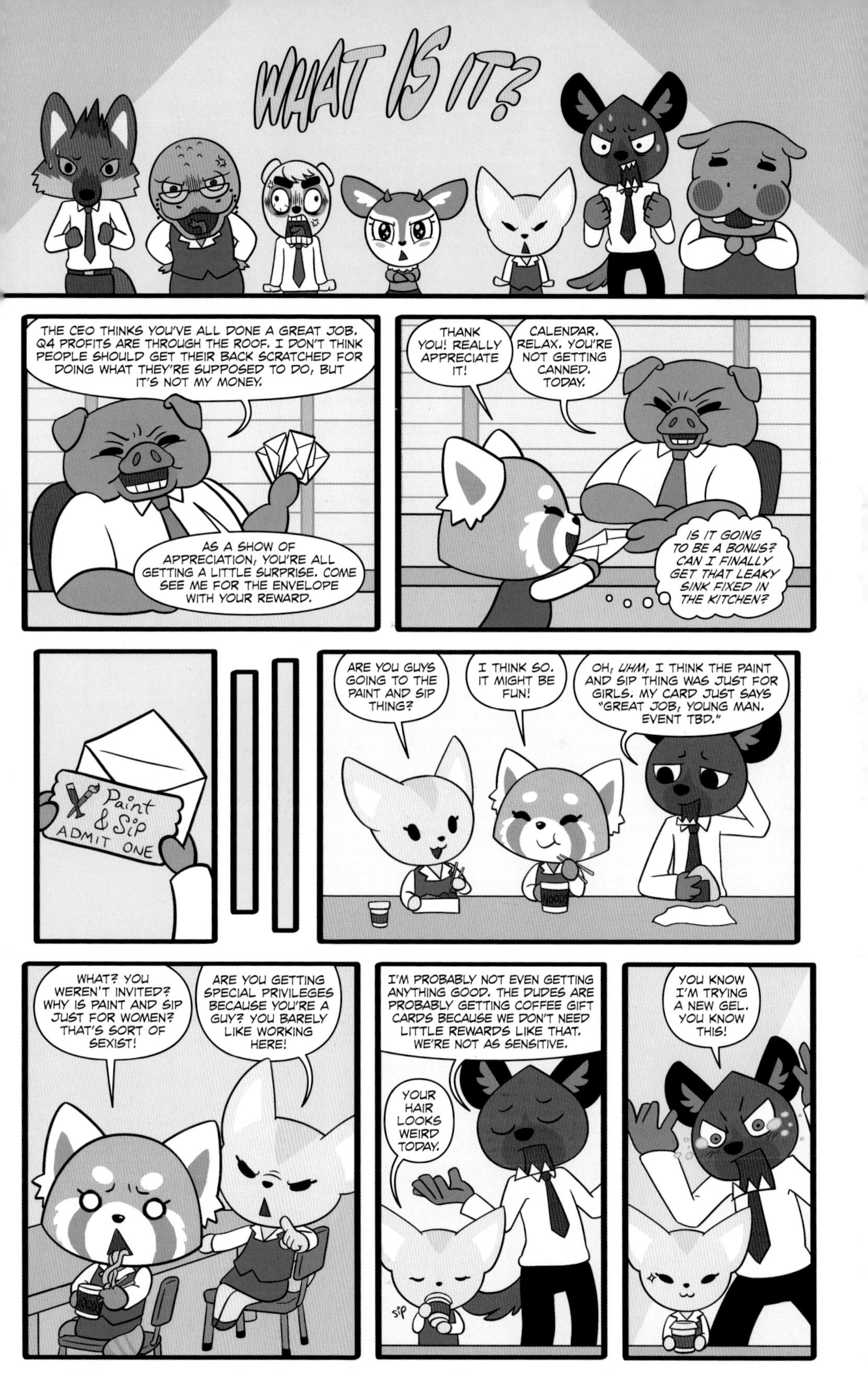
WHAT IS IT?
THE CEO THINKS YOU'VE ALL DONE A GREAT JOB. Q4 PROFITS ARE THROUGH THE ROOF. I DON'T THINK PEOPLE SHOULD GET THEIR BACK SCRATCHED FOR DOING WHAT THEY'RE SUPPOSED TO DO, BUT IT'S NOT MY MONEY.
AS A SHOW OF APPRECIATION, YOU'RE ALL GETTING A LITTLE SURPRISE. COME SEE ME FOR THE ENVELOPE WITH YOUR REWARD.
THANK YOU! REALLY APPRECIATE IT!
CALENDAR. RELAX. YOU'RE NOT GETTING CANNED. TODAY.
IS IT GOING TO BE A BONUS? CAN I FINALLY GET THAT LEAKY SINK FIXED IN THE KITCHEN?
Paint & Sip ADMIT ONE
ARE YOU GUYS GOING TO THE PAINT AND SIP THING?
I THINK SO. IT MIGHT BE FUN!
OH, UHM, I THINK THE PAINT AND SIP THING WAS JUST FOR GIRLS. MY CARD JUST SAYS "GREAT JOB, YOUNG MAN. EVENT TBD."
WHAT? YOU WEREN'T INVITED? WHY IS PAINT AND SIP JUST FOR WOMEN? THAT'S SORT OF SEXIST!
ARE YOU GETTING SPECIAL PRIVILEGES BECAUSE YOU'RE A GUY? YOU BARELY LIKE WORKING HERE!
I'M PROBABLY NOT EVEN GETTING ANYTHING GOOD. THE DUDES ARE PROBABLY GETTING COFFEE GIFT CARDS BECAUSE WE DON'T NEED LITTLE REWARDS LIKE THAT. WE'RE NOT AS SENSITIVE.
YOUR HAIR LOOKS WEIRD TODAY.
SIP
YOU KNOW I'M TRYING A NEW GEL. YOU KNOW THIS!

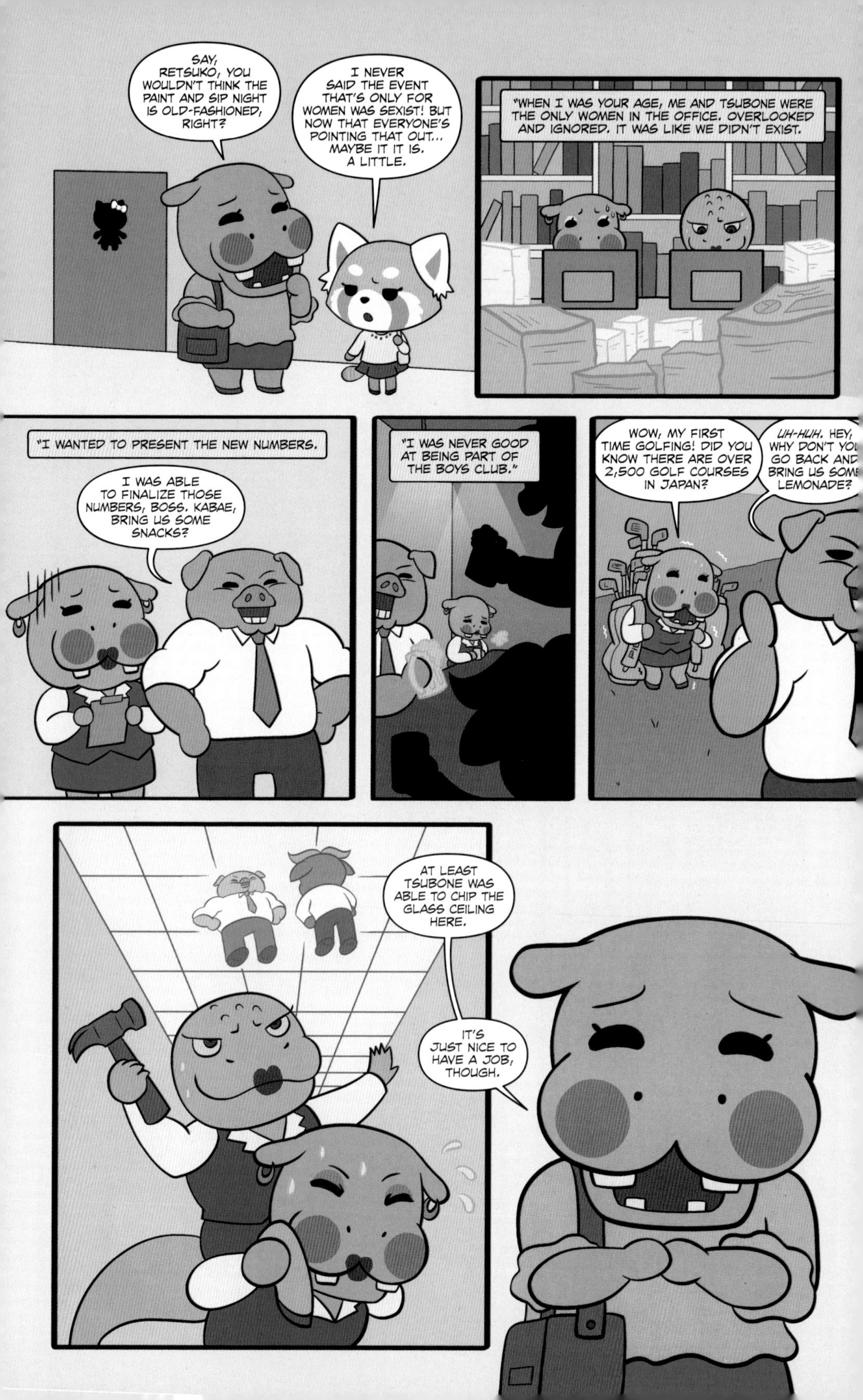
SAY, RETSUKO, YOU WOULDN'T THINK THE PAINT AND SIP NIGHT IS OLD-FASHIONED, RIGHT?
I NEVER SAID THE EVENT THAT'S ONLY FOR WOMEN WAS SEXIST! BUT NOW THAT EVERYONE'S POINTING THAT OUT... MAYBE IT IT IS. A LITTLE.
"WHEN I WAS YOUR AGE, ME AND TSUBONE WERE THE ONLY WOMEN IN THE OFFICE. OVERLOOKED AND IGNORED. IT WAS LIKE WE DIDN'T EXIST.
"I WANTED TO PRESENT THE NEW NUMBERS.
I WAS ABLE TO FINALIZE THOSE NUMBERS, BOSS. KABAE, BRING US SOME SNACKS?
"I WAS NEVER GOOD AT BEING PART OF THE BOYS CLUB."
WOW, MY FIRST TIME GOLFING! DID YOU KNOW THERE ARE OVER 2,500 GOLF COURSES IN JAPAN?
UH-HUH. HEY, WHY DON'T YOU GO BACK AND BRING US SOME LEMONADE?
AT LEAST TSUBONE WAS ABLE TO CHIP THE GLASS CEILING HERE.
IT'S JUST NICE TO HAVE A JOB, THOUGH.

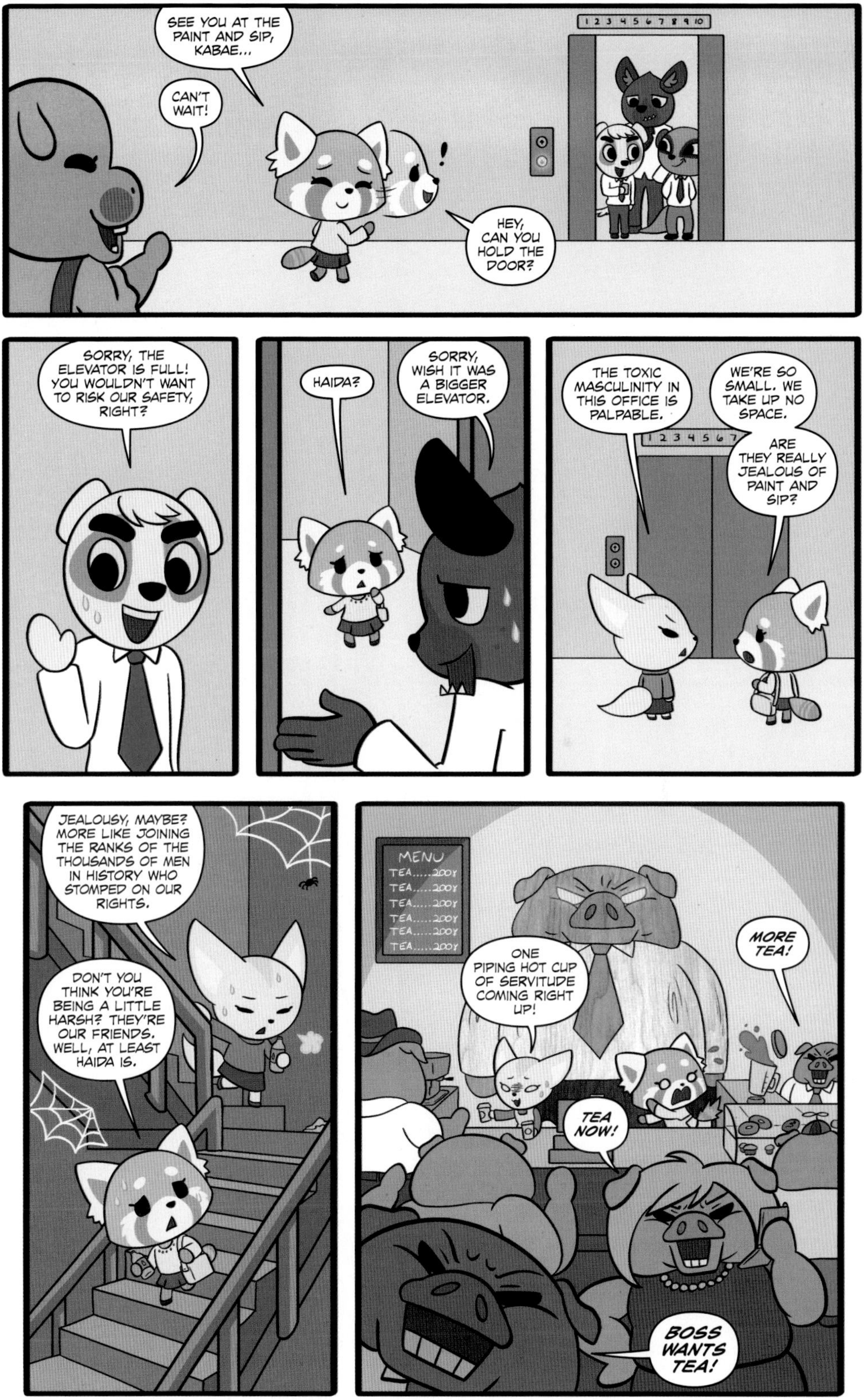
SEE YOU AT THE PAINT AND SIP, KABAE...
CAN'T WAIT!
HEY, CAN YOU HOLD THE DOOR?
SORRY, THE ELEVATOR IS FULL! YOU WOULDN'T WANT TO RISK OUR SAFETY, RIGHT?
HAIDA?
SORRY, WISH IT WAS A BIGGER ELEVATOR.
THE TOXIC MASCULINITY IN THIS OFFICE IS PALPABLE.
WE'RE SO SMALL. WE TAKE UP NO SPACE.
ARE THEY REALLY JEALOUS OF PAINT AND SIP?
JEALOUSY, MAYBE? MORE LIKE JOINING THE RANKS OF THE THOUSANDS OF MEN IN HISTORY WHO STOMPED ON OUR RIGHTS.
DON'T YOU THINK YOU'RE BEING A LITTLE HARSH? THEY'RE OUR FRIENDS. WELL, AT LEAST HAIDA IS.
MENU
TEA.....200¥
TEA.....200¥
TEA.....200¥
TEA.....200¥
TEA.....200¥
TEA.....200¥
ONE PIPING HOT CUP OF SERVITUDE COMING RIGHT UP!
MORE TEA!
TEA NOW!
BOSS WANTS TEA!

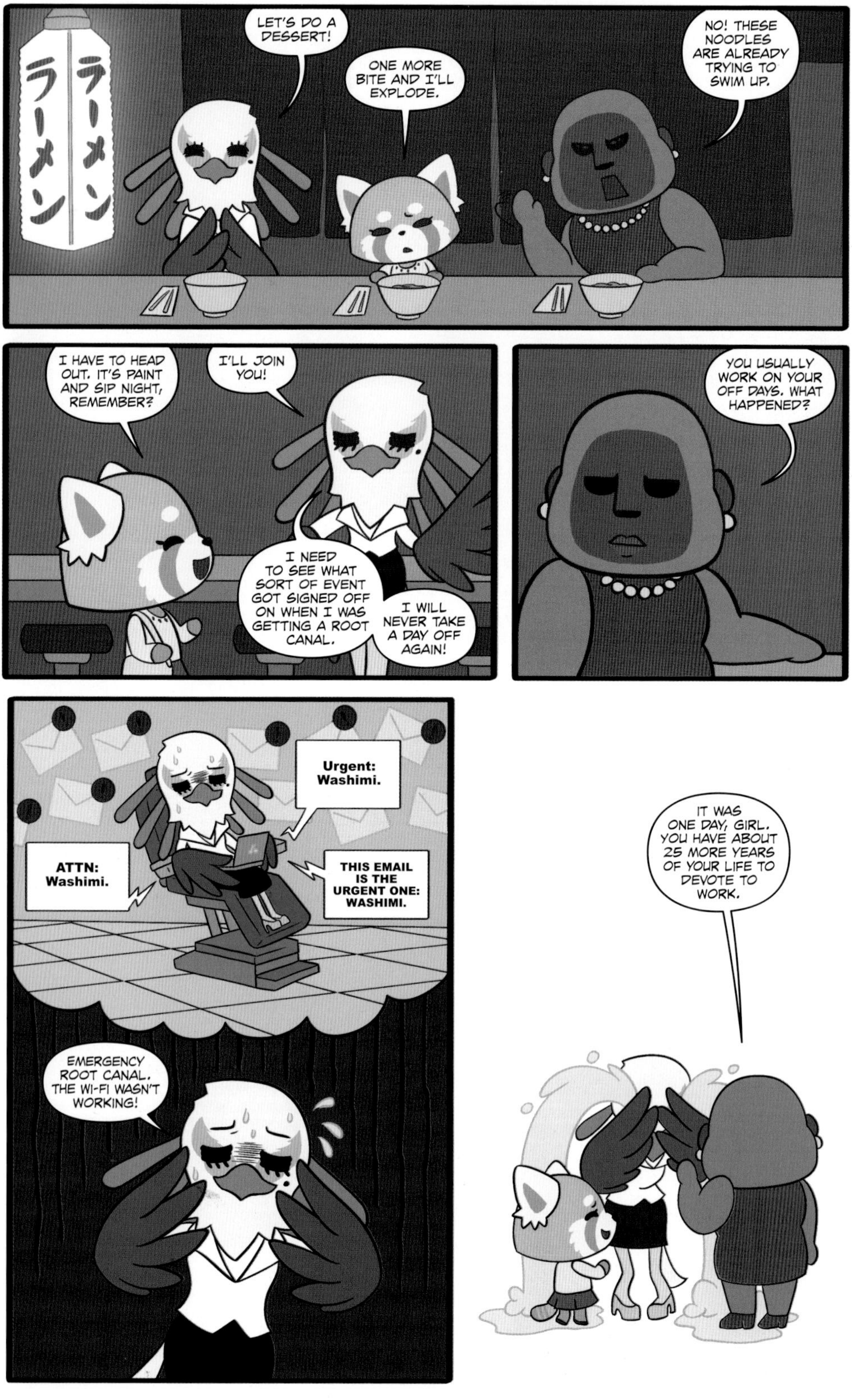
ラーメン
ラーメン
LET'S DO A DESSERT!
ONE MORE BITE AND I'LL EXPLODE.
NO! THESE NOODLES ARE ALREADY TRYING TO SWIM UP.
I HAVE TO HEAD OUT. IT'S PAINT AND SIP NIGHT, REMEMBER?
I'LL JOIN YOU!
I NEED TO SEE WHAT SORT OF EVENT GOT SIGNED OFF ON WHEN I WAS GETTING A ROOT CANAL.
I WILL NEVER TAKE A DAY OFF AGAIN!
YOU USUALLY WORK ON YOUR OFF DAYS. WHAT HAPPENED?
Urgent: Washimi.
ATTN: Washimi.
THIS EMAIL IS THE URGENT ONE: WASHIMI.
EMERGENCY ROOT CANAL. THE WI-FI WASN'T WORKING!
IT WAS ONE DAY, GIRL. YOU HAVE ABOUT 25 MORE YEARS OF YOUR LIFE TO DEVOTE TO WORK.

PAINT AND SIP NIGHT. THE NIGHT THE LADIES WILL PAINT. AND ALSO SIP.

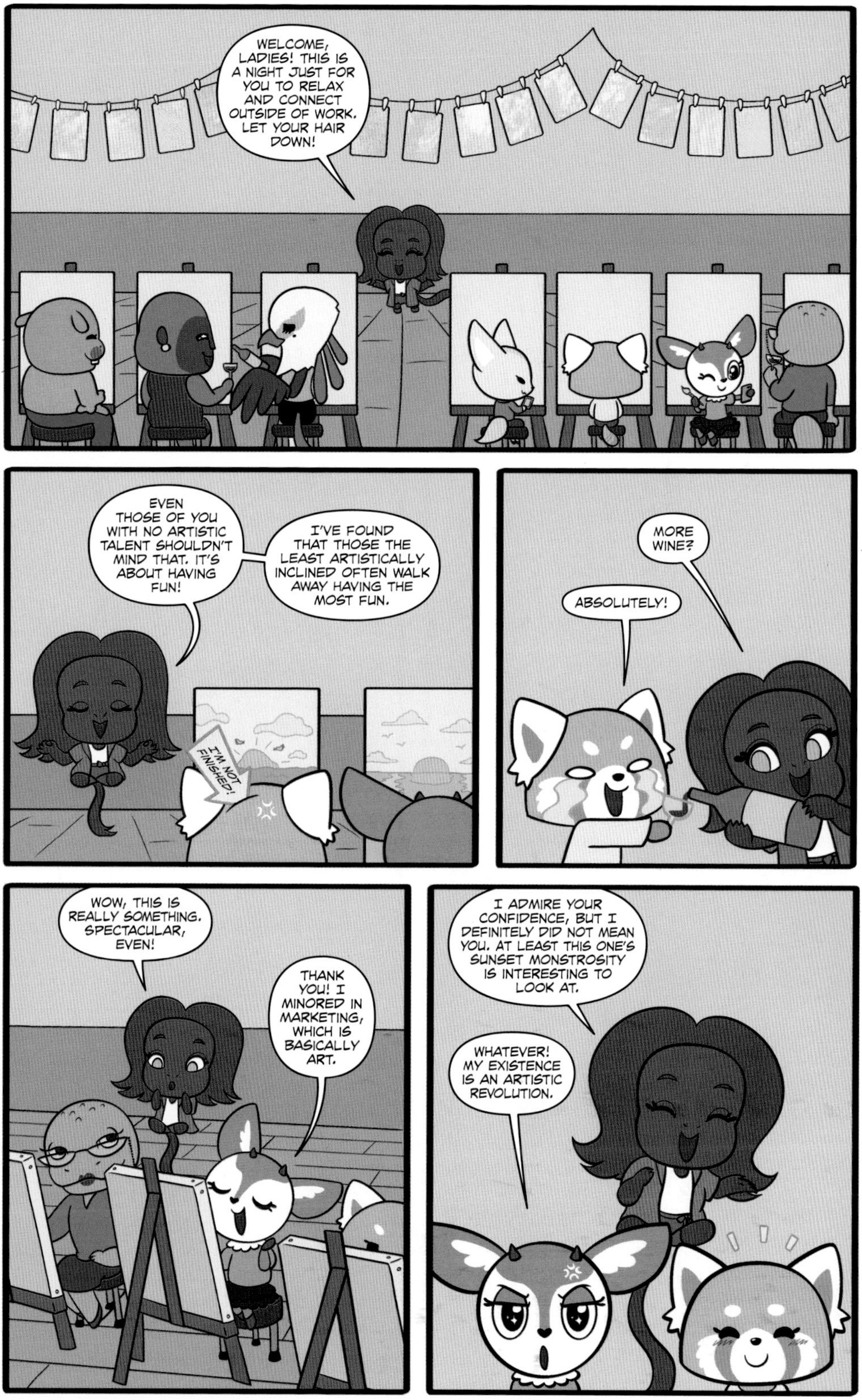
WELCOME, LADIES! THIS IS A NIGHT JUST FOR YOU TO RELAX AND CONNECT OUTSIDE OF WORK. LET YOUR HAIR DOWN!
EVEN THOSE OF YOU WITH NO ARTISTIC TALENT SHOULDN'T MIND THAT. IT'S ABOUT HAVING FUN!
I'VE FOUND THAT THOSE THE LEAST ARTISTICALLY INCLINED OFTEN WALK AWAY HAVING THE MOST FUN.
I'M NOT FINISHED!
MORE WINE?
ABSOLUTELY!
WOW, THIS IS REALLY SOMETHING. SPECTACULAR, EVEN!
THANK YOU! I MINORED IN MARKETING, WHICH IS BASICALLY ART.
I ADMIRE YOUR CONFIDENCE, BUT I DEFINITELY DID NOT MEAN YOU. AT LEAST THIS ONE'S SUNSET MONSTROSITY IS INTERESTING TO LOOK AT.
WHATEVER! MY EXISTENCE IS AN ARTISTIC REVOLUTION.

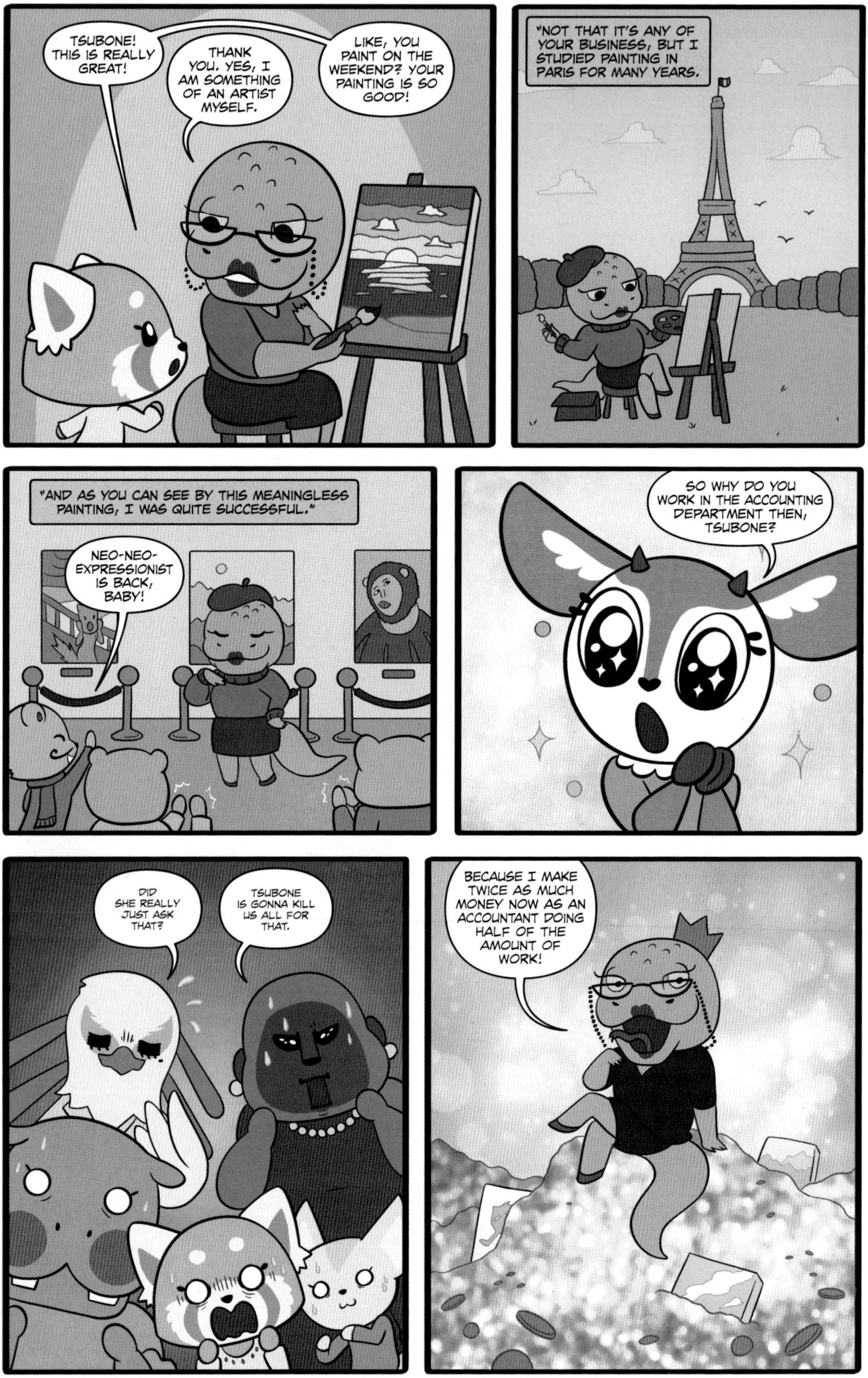
TSUBONE! THIS IS REALLY GREAT!
THANK YOU. YES, I AM SOMETHING OF AN ARTIST MYSELF.
LIKE, YOU PAINT ON THE WEEKEND? YOUR PAINTING IS SO GOOD!
"NOT THAT IT'S ANY OF YOUR BUSINESS, BUT I STUDIED PAINTING IN PARIS FOR MANY YEARS.
"AND AS YOU CAN SEE BY THIS MEANINGLESS PAINTING, I WAS QUITE SUCCESSFUL."
NEO-NEO-EXPRESSIONIST IS BACK, BABY!
SO WHY DO YOU WORK IN THE ACCOUNTING DEPARTMENT THEN, TSUBONE?
DID SHE REALLY JUST ASK THAT?
TSUBONE IS GONNA KILL US ALL FOR THAT.
BECAUSE I MAKE TWICE AS MUCH MONEY NOW AS AN ACCOUNTANT DOING HALF OF THE AMOUNT OF WORK!

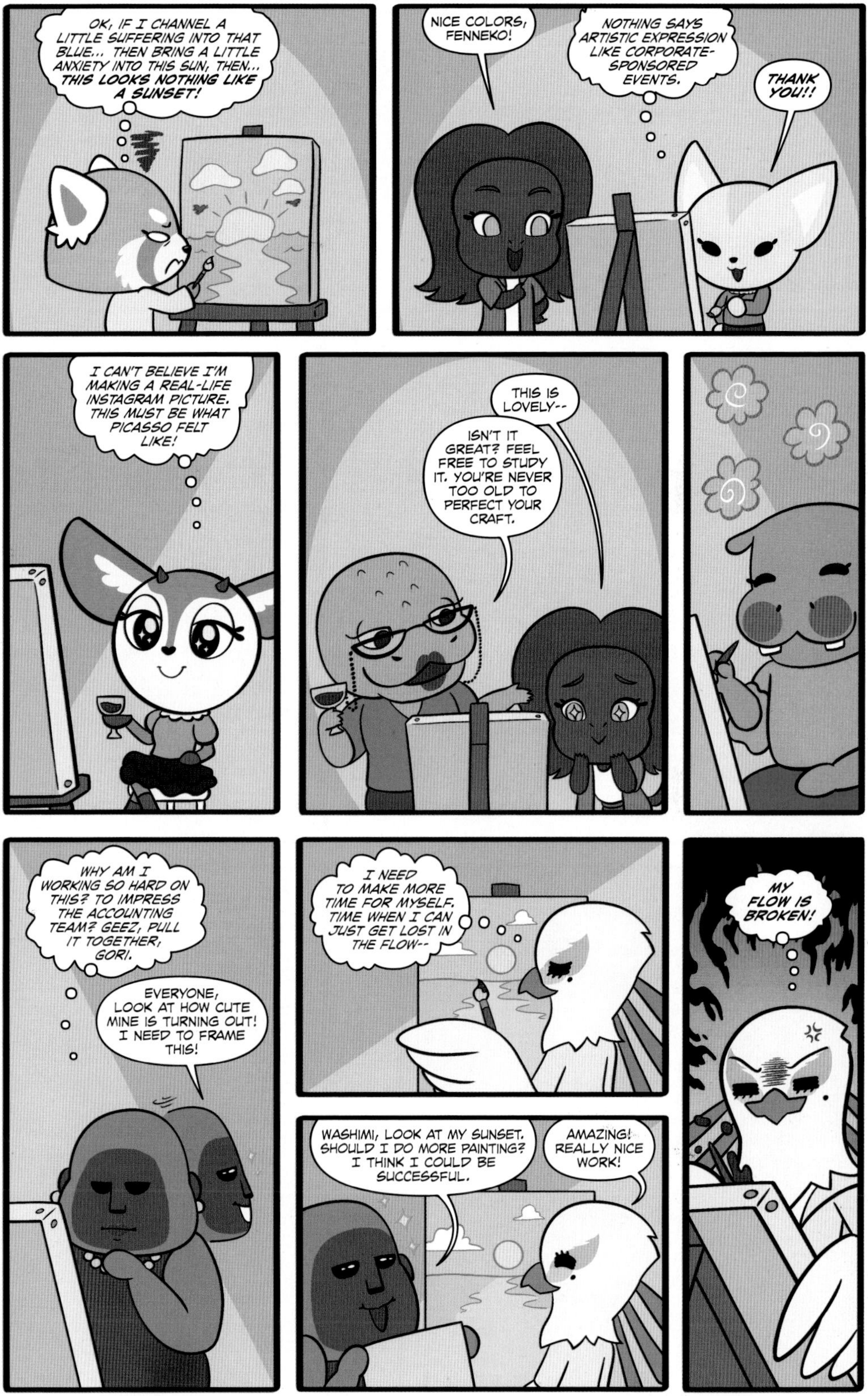
OK, IF I CHANNEL A LITTLE SUFFERING INTO THAT BLUE... THEN BRING A LITTLE ANXIETY INTO THIS SUN, THEN... THIS LOOKS NOTHING LIKE A SUNSET!
NICE COLORS, FENNEKO!
NOTHING SAYS ARTISTIC EXPRESSION LIKE CORPORATE-SPONSORED EVENTS.
THANK YOU!!
I CAN'T BELIEVE I'M MAKING A REAL-LIFE INSTAGRAM PICTURE. THIS MUST BE WHAT PICASSO FELT LIKE!
THIS IS LOVELY--
ISN'T IT GREAT? FEEL FREE TO STUDY IT. YOU'RE NEVER TOO OLD TO PERFECT YOUR CRAFT.
WHY AM I WORKING SO HARD ON THIS? TO IMPRESS THE ACCOUNTING TEAM? GEEZ, PULL IT TOGETHER, GORI.
EVERYONE, LOOK AT HOW CUTE MINE IS TURNING OUT! I NEED TO FRAME THIS!
I NEED TO MAKE MORE TIME FOR MYSELF. TIME WHEN I CAN JUST GET LOST IN THE FLOW--
WASHIMI, LOOK AT MY SUNSET. SHOULD I DO MORE PAINTING? I THINK I COULD BE SUCCESSFUL.
AMAZING! REALLY NICE WORK!
MY FLOW IS BROKEN!

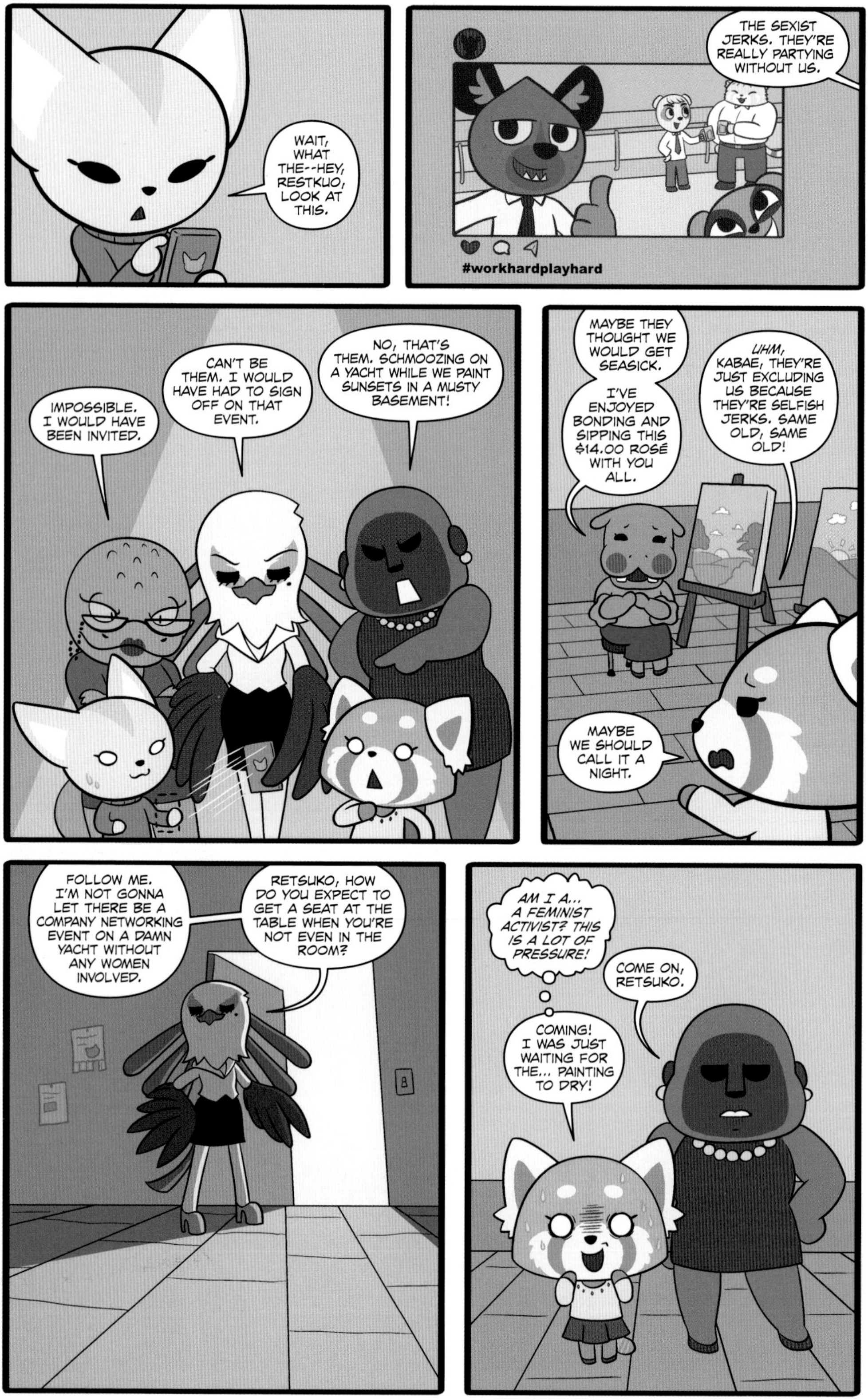
WAIT, WHAT THE--HEY, RESTKUO, LOOK AT THIS.
THE SEXIST JERKS. THEY'RE REALLY PARTYING WITHOUT US.
#workhardplayhard
IMPOSSIBLE. I WOULD HAVE BEEN INVITED.
CAN'T BE THEM. I WOULD HAVE HAD TO SIGN OFF ON THAT EVENT.
NO, THAT'S THEM. SCHMOOZING ON A YACHT WHILE WE PAINT SUNSETS IN A MUSTY BASEMENT!
MAYBE THEY THOUGHT WE WOULD GET SEASICK.
I'VE ENJOYED BONDING AND SIPPING THIS $14.00 ROSÉ WITH YOU ALL.
UHM, KABAE, THEY'RE JUST EXCLUDING US BECAUSE THEY'RE SELFISH JERKS. SAME OLD, SAME OLD!
MAYBE WE SHOULD CALL IT A NIGHT.
FOLLOW ME. I'M NOT GONNA LET THERE BE A COMPANY NETWORKING EVENT ON A DAMN YACHT WITHOUT ANY WOMEN INVOLVED.
RETSUKO, HOW DO YOU EXPECT TO GET A SEAT AT THE TABLE WHEN YOU'RE NOT EVEN IN THE ROOM?
AM I A... A FEMINIST ACTIVIST? THIS IS A LOT OF PRESSURE!
COME ON, RETSUKO.
COMING! I WAS JUST WAITING FOR THE... PAINTING TO DRY!

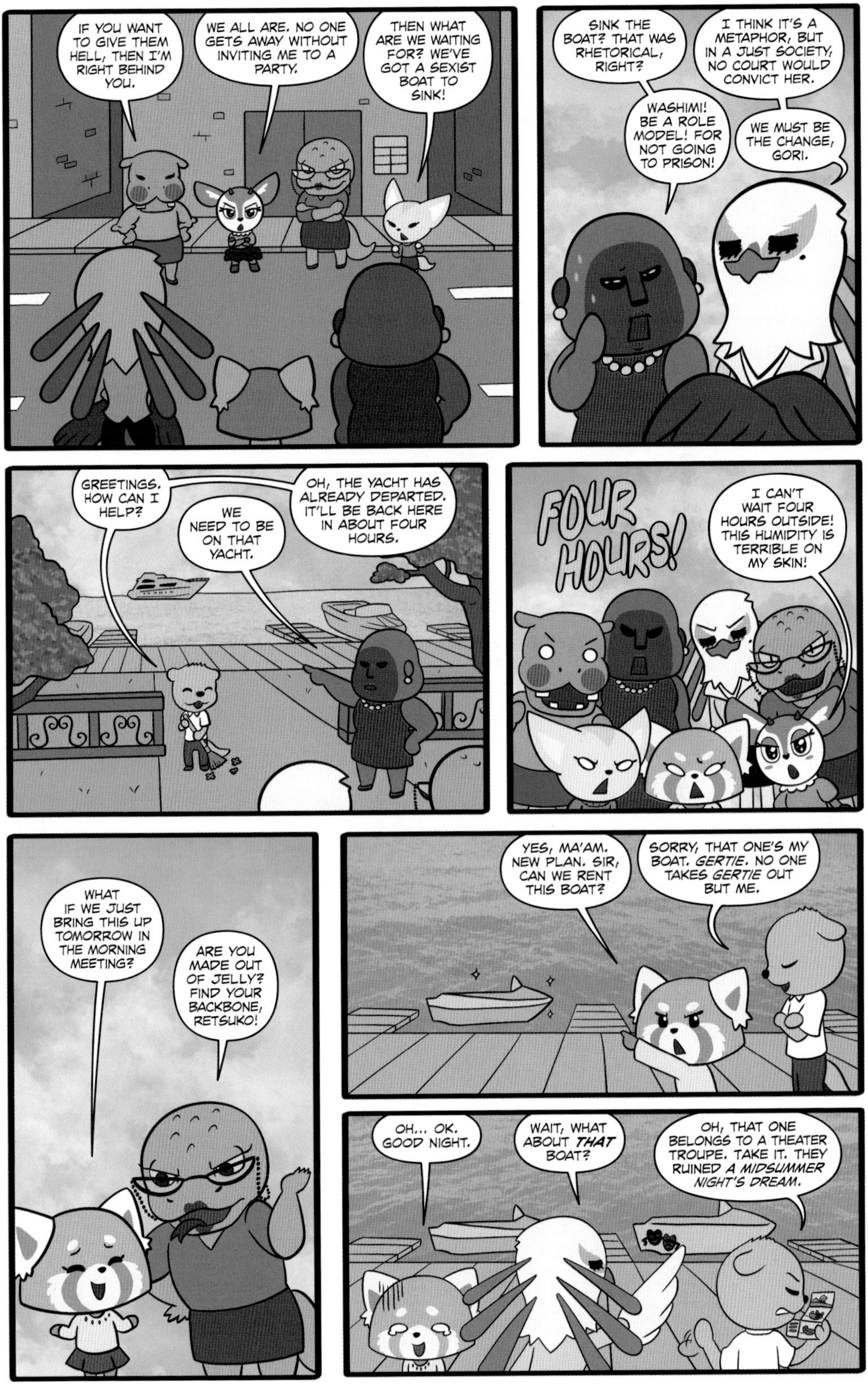
IF YOU WANT TO GIVE THEM HELL, THEN I'M RIGHT BEHIND YOU.
WE ALL ARE. NO ONE GETS AWAY WITHOUT INVITING ME TO A PARTY.
THEN WHAT ARE WE WAITING FOR? WE'VE GOT A SEXIST BOAT TO SINK!
SINK THE BOAT? THAT WAS RHETORICAL, RIGHT?
I THINK IT'S A METAPHOR, BUT IN A JUST SOCIETY, NO COURT WOULD CONVICT HER.
WASHIMI! BE A ROLE MODEL! FOR NOT GOING TO PRISON!
WE MUST BE THE CHANGE, GORI.
GREETINGS. HOW CAN I HELP?
WE NEED TO BE ON THAT YACHT.
OH, THE YACHT HAS ALREADY DEPARTED. IT'LL BE BACK HERE IN ABOUT FOUR HOURS.
FOUR HOURS!
I CAN'T WAIT FOUR HOURS OUTSIDE! THIS HUMIDITY IS TERRIBLE ON MY SKIN!
WHAT IF WE JUST BRING THIS UP TOMORROW IN THE MORNING MEETING?
ARE YOU MADE OUT OF JELLY? FIND YOUR BACKBONE, RETSUKO!
YES, MA'AM. NEW PLAN. SIR, CAN WE RENT THIS BOAT?
SORRY, THAT ONE'S MY BOAT. *GERTIE*. NO ONE TAKES *GERTIE* OUT BUT ME.
OH... OK. GOOD NIGHT.
WAIT, WHAT ABOUT *THAT* BOAT?
OH, THAT ONE BELONGS TO A THEATER TROUPE. TAKE IT. THEY RUINED *A MIDSUMMER NIGHT'S DREAM*.

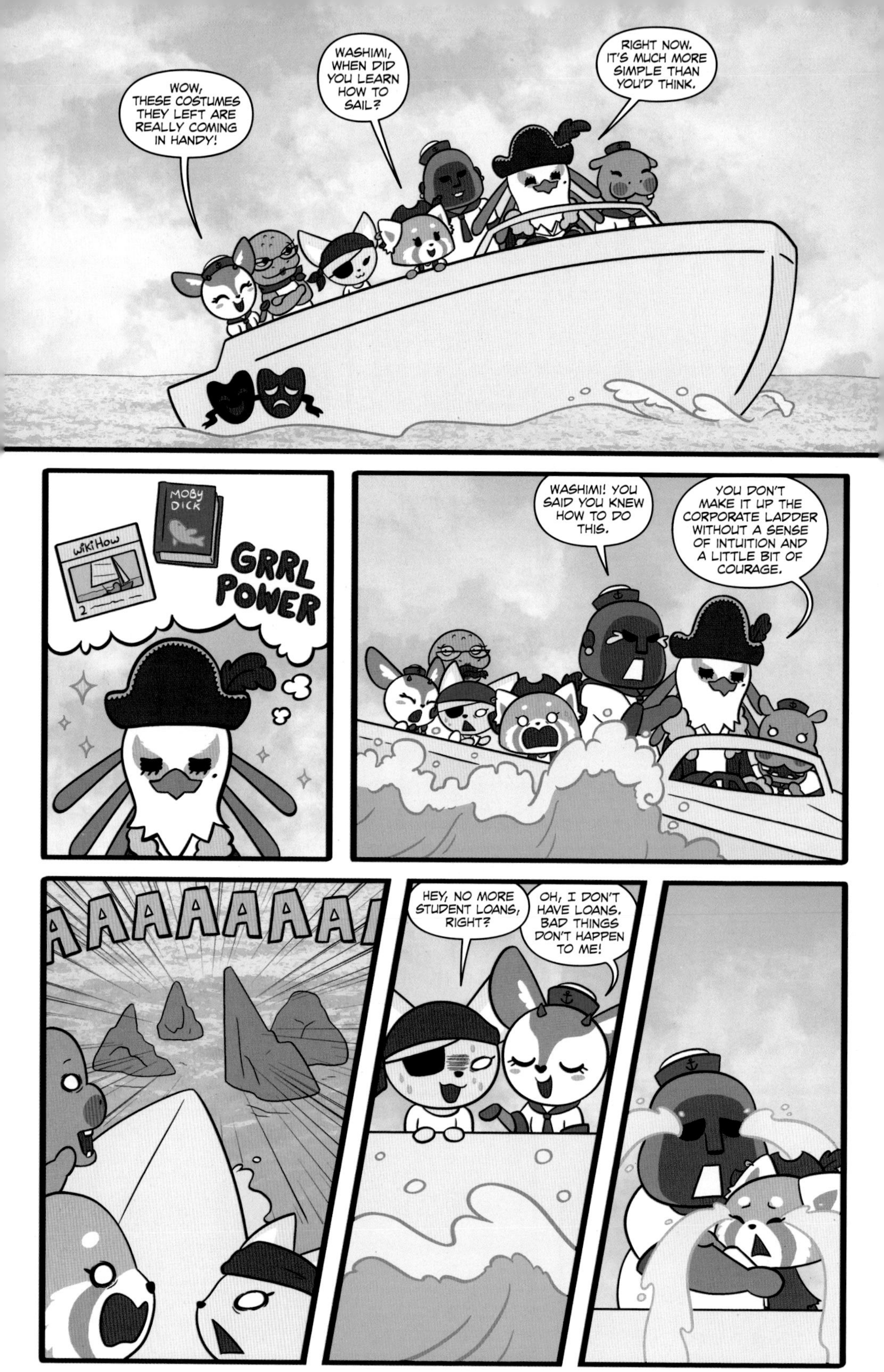

WOW, THESE COSTUMES THEY LEFT ARE REALLY COMING IN HANDY!
WASHIMI, WHEN DID YOU LEARN HOW TO SAIL?
RIGHT NOW. IT'S MUCH MORE SIMPLE THAN YOU'D THINK.
MOBY DICK
wikiHow
GRRL POWER
WASHIMI! YOU SAID YOU KNEW HOW TO DO THIS.
YOU DON'T MAKE IT UP THE CORPORATE LADDER WITHOUT A SENSE OF INTUITION AND A LITTLE BIT OF COURAGE.
AAAAAAAA
HEY, NO MORE STUDENT LOANS, RIGHT?
OH, I DON'T HAVE LOANS. BAD THINGS DON'T HAPPEN TO ME!

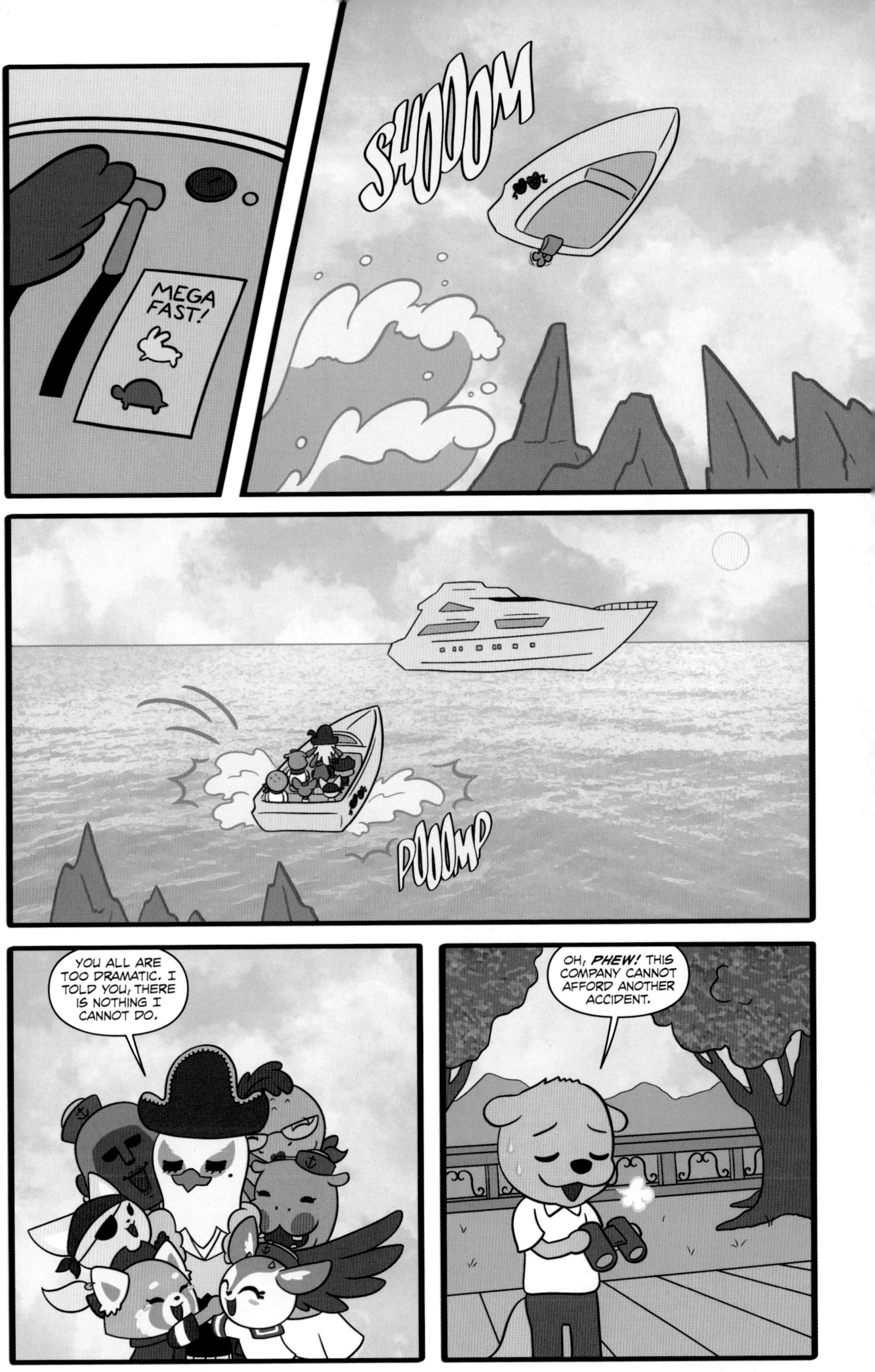
MEGA FAST!
SHOOOM
POOOMP
YOU ALL ARE TOO DRAMATIC. I TOLD YOU, THERE IS NOTHING I CANNOT DO.
OH, PHEW! THIS COMPANY CANNOT AFFORD ANOTHER ACCIDENT.

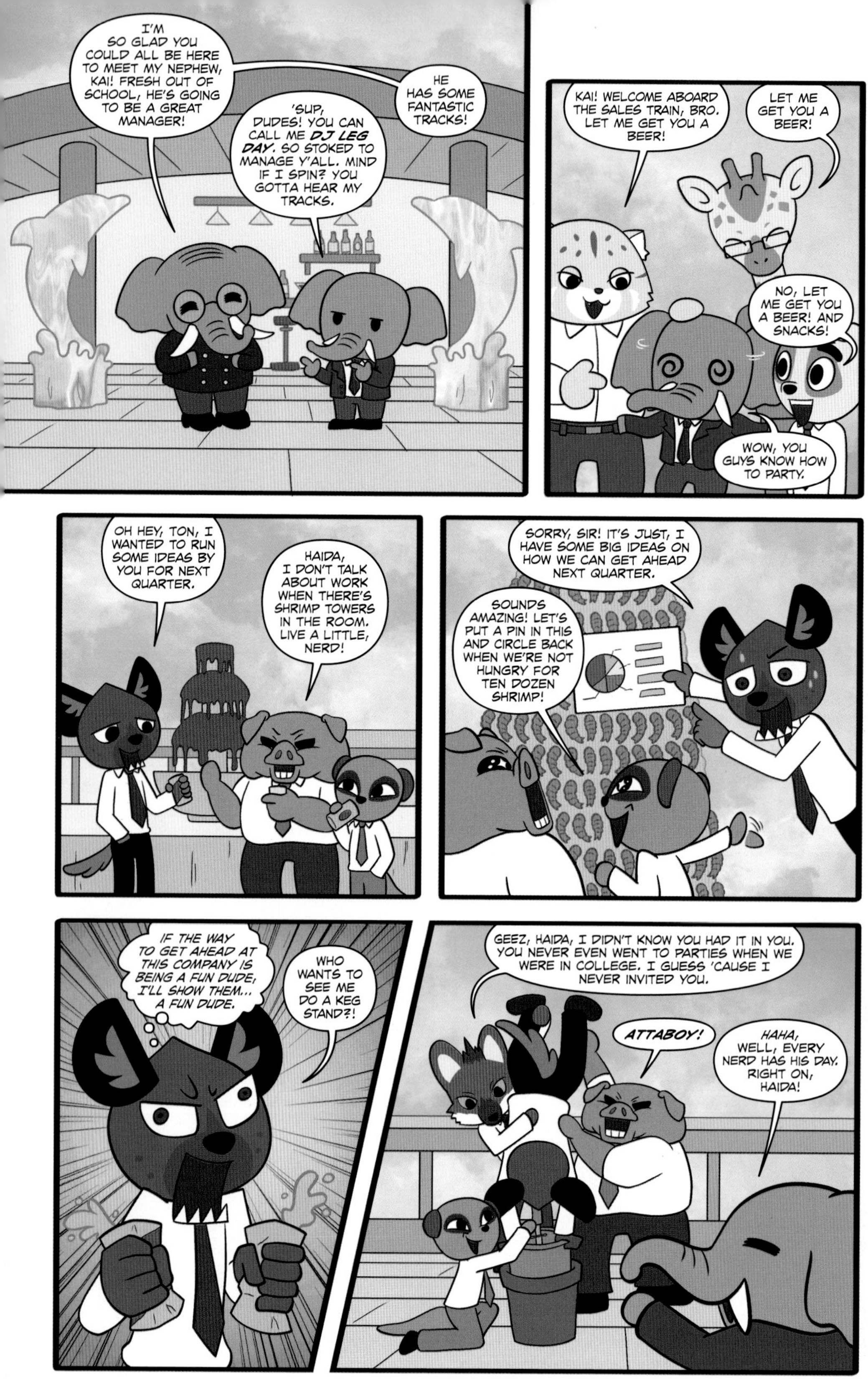
I'M SO GLAD YOU COULD ALL BE HERE TO MEET MY NEPHEW, KAI! FRESH OUT OF SCHOOL, HE'S GOING TO BE A GREAT MANAGER!
HE HAS SOME FANTASTIC TRACKS!
'SUP, DUDES! YOU CAN CALL ME DJ LEG DAY. SO STOKED TO MANAGE Y'ALL. MIND IF I SPIN? YOU GOTTA HEAR MY TRACKS.
KAI! WELCOME ABOARD THE SALES TRAIN, BRO. LET ME GET YOU A BEER!
LET ME GET YOU A BEER!
NO, LET ME GET YOU A BEER! AND SNACKS!
WOW, YOU GUYS KNOW HOW TO PARTY.
OH HEY, TON, I WANTED TO RUN SOME IDEAS BY YOU FOR NEXT QUARTER.
HAIDA, I DON'T TALK ABOUT WORK WHEN THERE'S SHRIMP TOWERS IN THE ROOM. LIVE A LITTLE, NERD!
SORRY, SIR! IT'S JUST, I HAVE SOME BIG IDEAS ON HOW WE CAN GET AHEAD NEXT QUARTER.
SOUNDS AMAZING! LET'S PUT A PIN IN THIS AND CIRCLE BACK WHEN WE'RE NOT HUNGRY FOR TEN DOZEN SHRIMP!
IF THE WAY TO GET AHEAD AT THIS COMPANY IS BEING A FUN DUDE, I'LL SHOW THEM... A FUN DUDE.
WHO WANTS TO SEE ME DO A KEG STAND?!
GEEZ, HAIDA, I DIDN'T KNOW YOU HAD IT IN YOU. YOU NEVER EVEN WENT TO PARTIES WHEN WE WERE IN COLLEGE. I GUESS 'CAUSE I NEVER INVITED YOU.
ATTABOY!
HAHA, WELL, EVERY NERD HAS HIS DAY. RIGHT ON, HAIDA!

HAIDA?!

CODE RED! FEMALE INTERLOPERS APPROACH. *CODE RED!*

WE'RE BEING INVADED!

LOOKS LIKE DOODLING FOR GIRLS ENDED TOO EARLY. WAY TOO EARLY.

SIR! SHALL I CUT THEIR ANCHOR SO THEY'LL FLOAT AWAY?

FORGET IT. JUST PROTECT OUR SHRIMP.

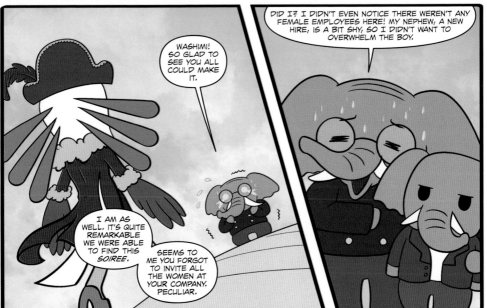

WASHIMI! SO GLAD TO SEE YOU ALL COULD MAKE IT.

DID I? I DIDN'T EVEN NOTICE THERE WEREN'T ANY FEMALE EMPLOYEES HERE! MY NEPHEW, A NEW HIRE, IS A BIT SHY, SO I DIDN'T WANT TO OVERWHELM THE BOY.

I AM AS WELL. IT'S QUITE REMARKABLE WE WERE ABLE TO FIND THIS *SOIREE.*

SEEMS TO ME YOU FORGOT TO INVITE ALL THE WOMEN AT YOUR COMPANY. PECULIAR.

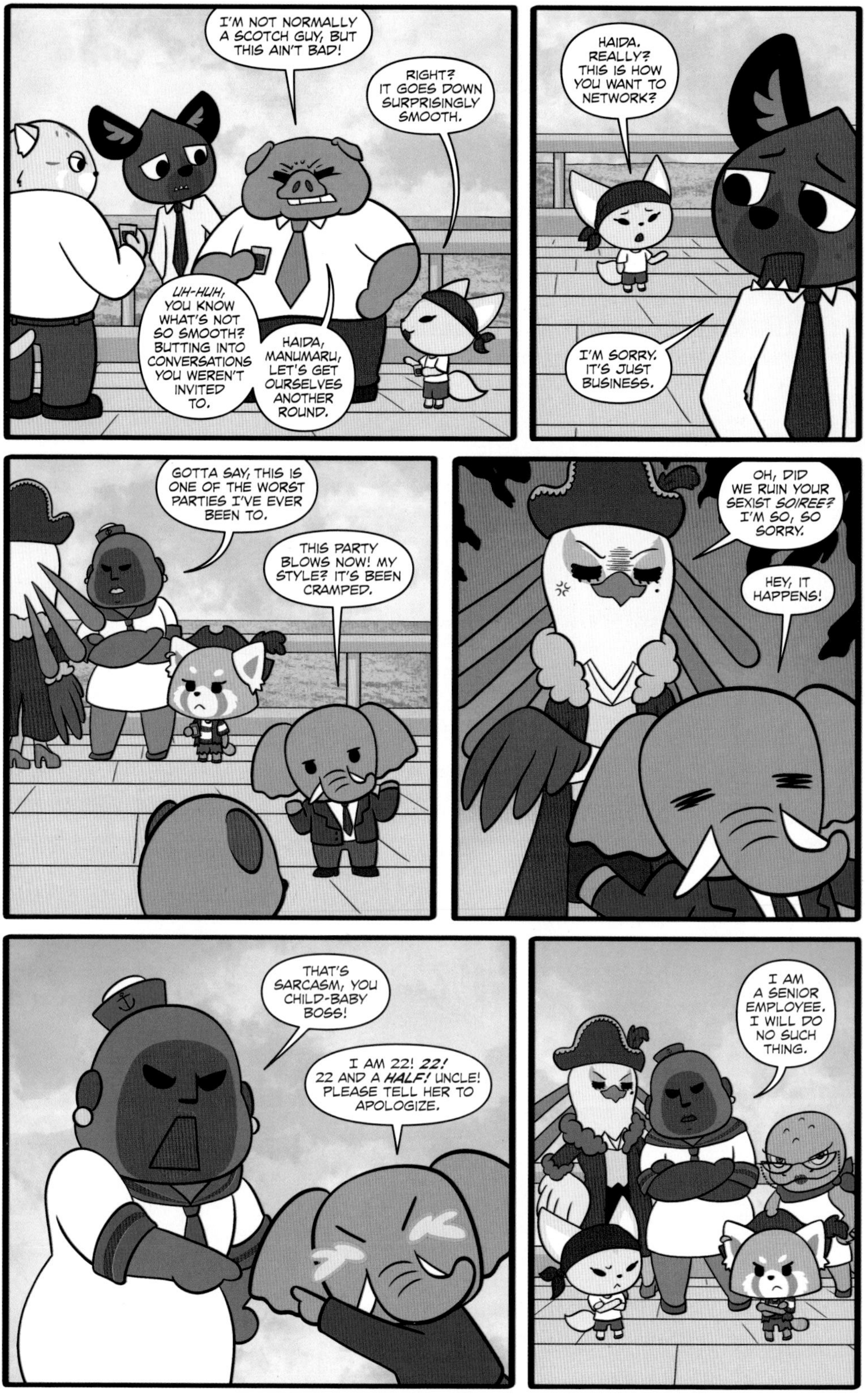
I'M NOT NORMALLY A SCOTCH GUY, BUT THIS AIN'T BAD!
RIGHT? IT GOES DOWN SURPRISINGLY SMOOTH.
UH-HUH, YOU KNOW WHAT'S NOT SO SMOOTH? BUTTING INTO CONVERSATIONS YOU WEREN'T INVITED TO.
HAIDA, MANUMARU, LET'S GET OURSELVES ANOTHER ROUND.
HAIDA. REALLY? THIS IS HOW YOU WANT TO NETWORK?
I'M SORRY. IT'S JUST BUSINESS.
GOTTA SAY, THIS IS ONE OF THE WORST PARTIES I'VE EVER BEEN TO.
THIS PARTY BLOWS NOW! MY STYLE? IT'S BEEN CRAMPED.
OH, DID WE RUIN YOUR SEXIST SOIREE? I'M SO, SO SORRY.
HEY, IT HAPPENS!
THAT'S SARCASM, YOU CHILD-BABY BOSS!
I AM 22! 22! 22 AND A HALF! UNCLE! PLEASE TELL HER TO APOLOGIZE.
I AM A SENIOR EMPLOYEE. I WILL DO NO SUCH THING.

EVERYONE, PLEASE! LET'S UNPACK THIS TOMORROW AT WORK. GUYS, I'M SO SORRY THE PARTY WAS RUINED.

I JUST THINK THINGS ARE GETTING A LITTLE ESCALATED. SOMETIMES PEOPLE GET EMOTIONAL!

YOU'RE APOLOGIZING TO THEM? I SHOULD CLEAN MY EARS, 'CAUSE THAT CAN'T BE WHAT I HEARD.

HEY NOW, THERE'S NOTHING WRONG WITH EMOTIONS. WE SHOULD BE FREE TO BE OURSELVES AT WORK, YOU KNOW.

STOP RUINING OUR NETWORKING TIME! I NEED A MENTOR!

YOUR BAD VIBES ARE DROWNING OUT MY BEATS, AKA MY GOOD VIBES.

NO ONE EVER OFFERED TO MENTOR ME!

OH RELAX! SOMEONE WOULD OFFER TO MENTOR YOU IF YOU WEREN'T SO MEDIOCRE!

EXCUSE ME... JUST GOING TO GO... THE RESTROOM.

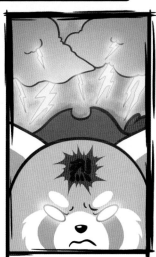

47

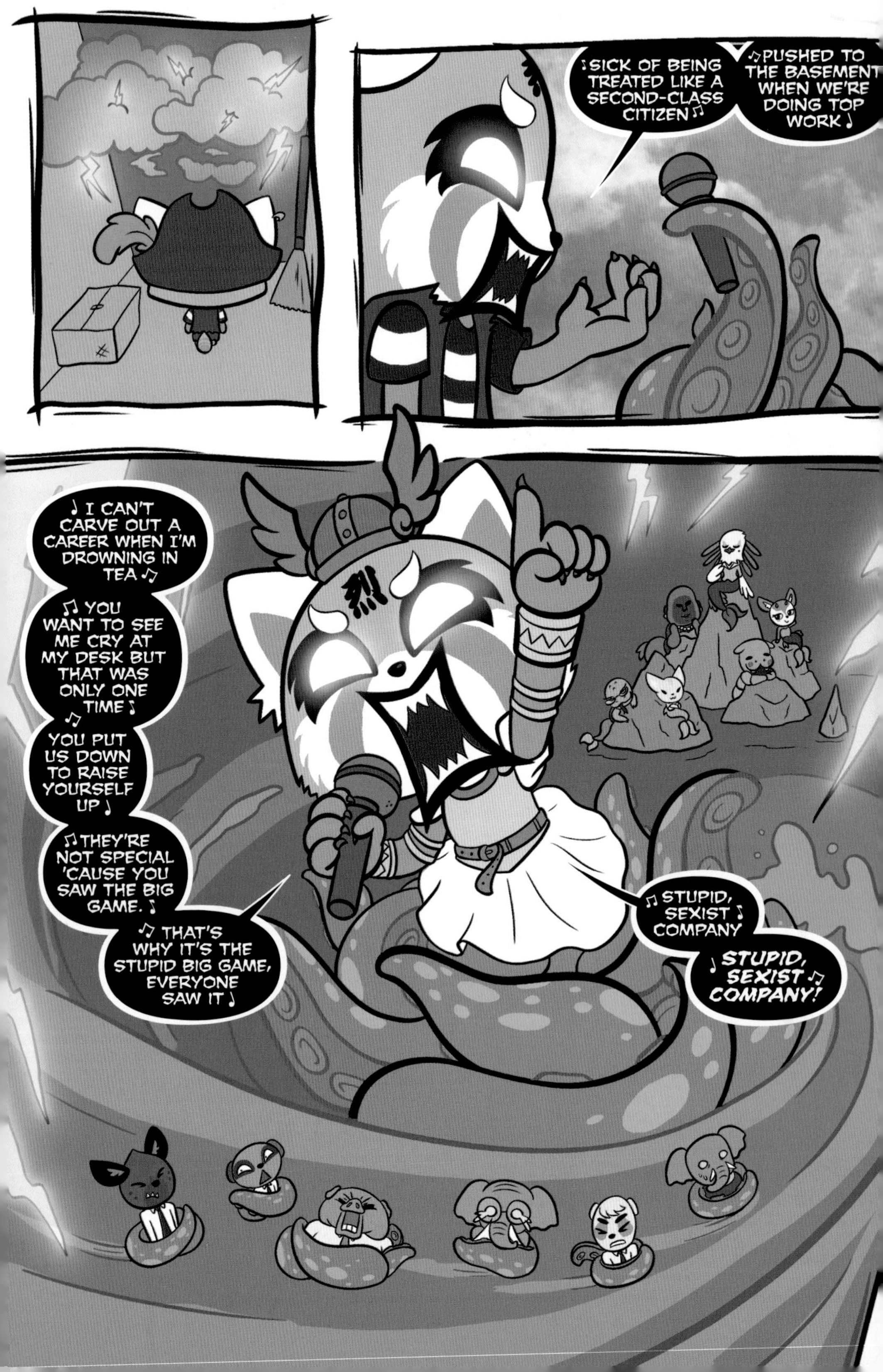
♪ SICK OF BEING TREATED LIKE A SECOND-CLASS CITIZEN ♫
♫ PUSHED TO THE BASEMENT WHEN WE'RE DOING TOP WORK ♪
♪ I CAN'T CARVE OUT A CAREER WHEN I'M DROWNING IN TEA ♫
♫ YOU WANT TO SEE ME CRY AT MY DESK BUT THAT WAS ONLY ONE TIME ♪
♫ YOU PUT US DOWN TO RAISE YOURSELF UP ♪
♫ THEY'RE NOT SPECIAL 'CAUSE YOU SAW THE BIG GAME. ♪
♫ THAT'S WHY IT'S THE STUPID BIG GAME, EVERYONE SAW IT ♪
♫ STUPID, SEXIST ♫ COMPANY
♪ STUPID, SEXIST ♫ COMPANY!

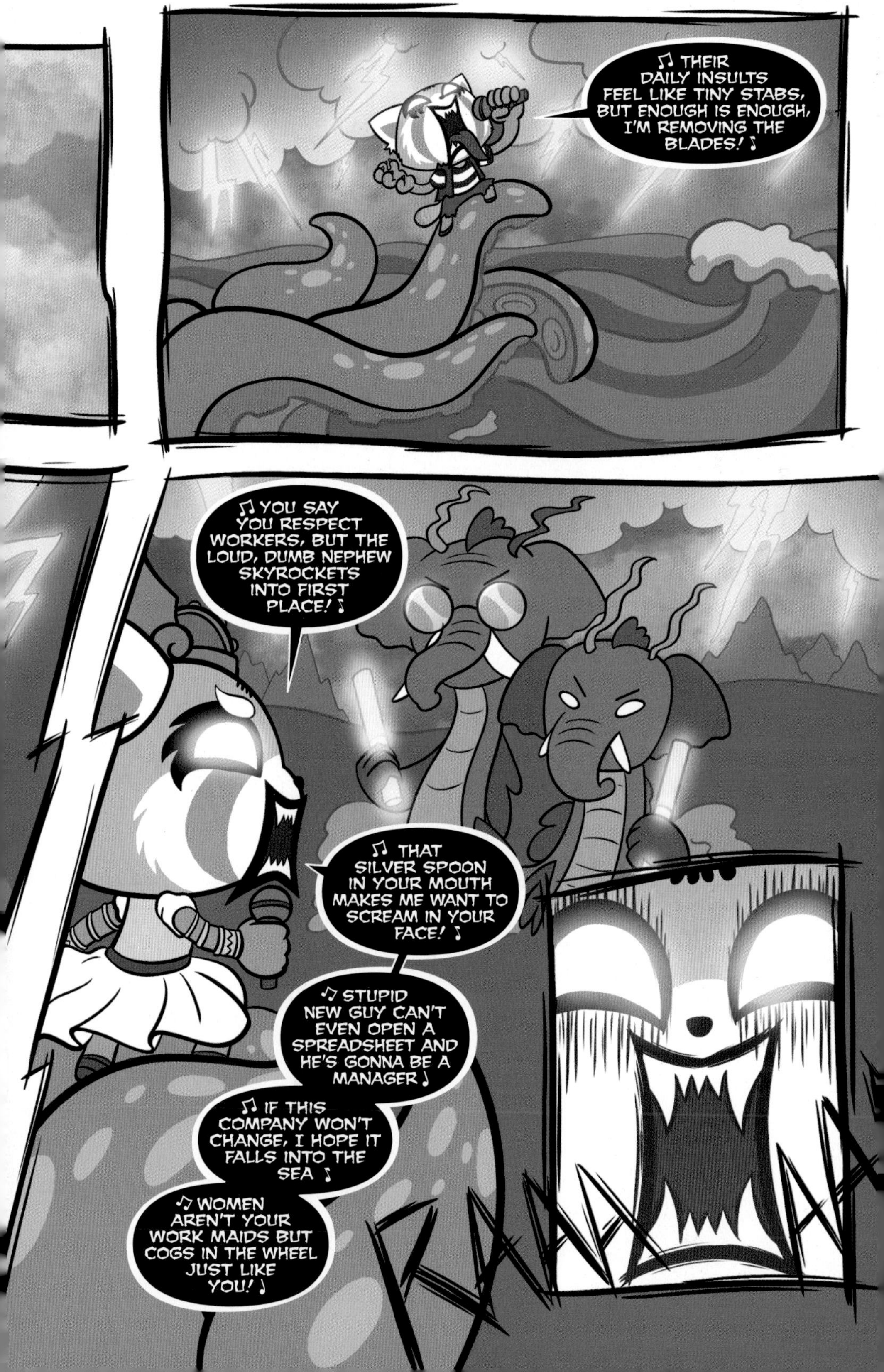
♫ THEIR DAILY INSULTS FEEL LIKE TINY STABS, BUT ENOUGH IS ENOUGH, I'M REMOVING THE BLADES! ♪
♫ YOU SAY YOU RESPECT WORKERS, BUT THE LOUD, DUMB NEPHEW SKYROCKETS INTO FIRST PLACE! ♪
♫ THAT SILVER SPOON IN YOUR MOUTH MAKES ME WANT TO SCREAM IN YOUR FACE! ♪
♫ STUPID NEW GUY CAN'T EVEN OPEN A SPREADSHEET AND HE'S GONNA BE A MANAGER ♪
♫ IF THIS COMPANY WON'T CHANGE, I HOPE IT FALLS INTO THE SEA ♪
♫ WOMEN AREN'T YOUR WORK MAIDS BUT COGS IN THE WHEEL JUST LIKE YOU! ♪

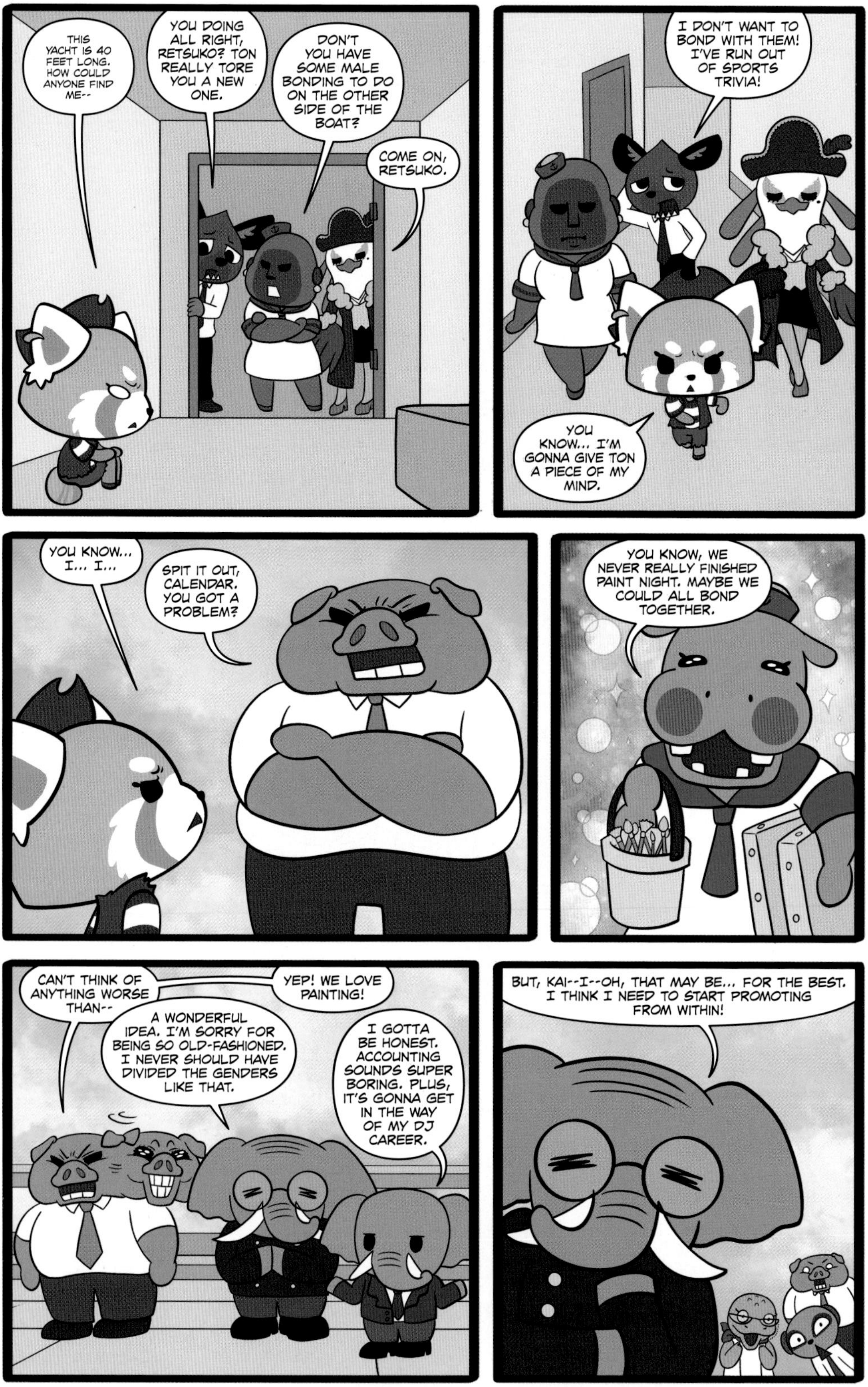
THIS YACHT IS 40 FEET LONG. HOW COULD ANYONE FIND ME--
YOU DOING ALL RIGHT, RETSUKO? TON REALLY TORE YOU A NEW ONE.
DON'T YOU HAVE SOME MALE BONDING TO DO ON THE OTHER SIDE OF THE BOAT?
COME ON, RETSUKO.
I DON'T WANT TO BOND WITH THEM! I'VE RUN OUT OF SPORTS TRIVIA!
YOU KNOW... I'M GONNA GIVE TON A PIECE OF MY MIND.
YOU KNOW... I... I...
SPIT IT OUT, CALENDAR. YOU GOT A PROBLEM?
YOU KNOW, WE NEVER REALLY FINISHED PAINT NIGHT. MAYBE WE COULD ALL BOND TOGETHER.
CAN'T THINK OF ANYTHING WORSE THAN--
YEP! WE LOVE PAINTING!
A WONDERFUL IDEA. I'M SORRY FOR BEING SO OLD-FASHIONED. I NEVER SHOULD HAVE DIVIDED THE GENDERS LIKE THAT.
I GOTTA BE HONEST. ACCOUNTING SOUNDS SUPER BORING. PLUS, IT'S GONNA GET IN THE WAY OF MY DJ CAREER.
BUT, KAI--I--OH, THAT MAY BE... FOR THE BEST. I THINK I NEED TO START PROMOTING FROM WITHIN!

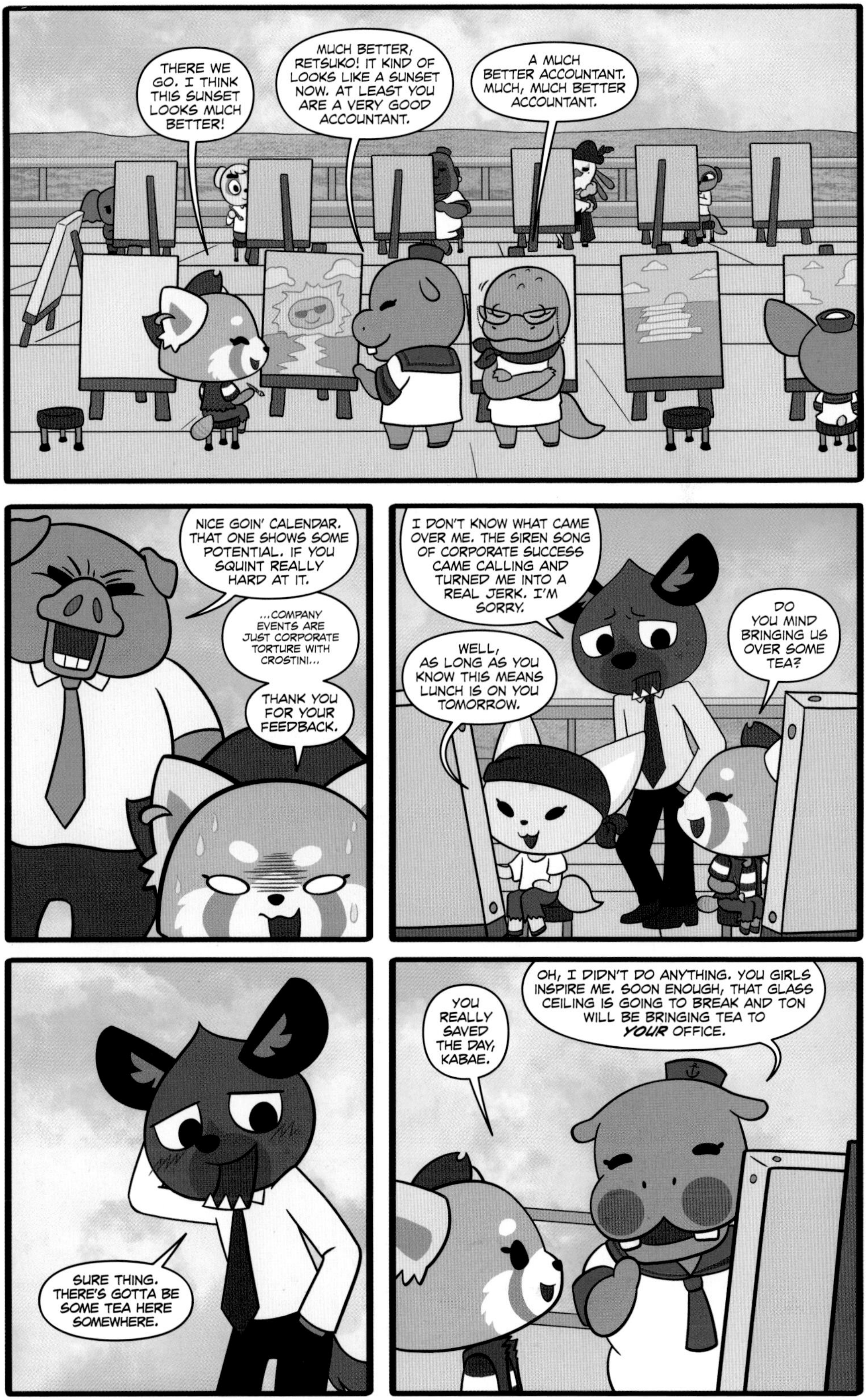
THERE WE GO. I THINK THIS SUNSET LOOKS MUCH BETTER!
MUCH BETTER, RETSUKO! IT KIND OF LOOKS LIKE A SUNSET NOW. AT LEAST YOU ARE A VERY GOOD ACCOUNTANT.
A MUCH BETTER ACCOUNTANT. MUCH, MUCH BETTER ACCOUNTANT.
NICE GOIN' CALENDAR. THAT ONE SHOWS SOME POTENTIAL. IF YOU SQUINT REALLY HARD AT IT.
...COMPANY EVENTS ARE JUST CORPORATE TORTURE WITH CROSTINI...
THANK YOU FOR YOUR FEEDBACK.
I DON'T KNOW WHAT CAME OVER ME. THE SIREN SONG OF CORPORATE SUCCESS CAME CALLING AND TURNED ME INTO A REAL JERK. I'M SORRY.
WELL, AS LONG AS YOU KNOW THIS MEANS LUNCH IS ON YOU TOMORROW.
DO YOU MIND BRINGING US OVER SOME TEA?
SURE THING. THERE'S GOTTA BE SOME TEA HERE SOMEWHERE.
YOU REALLY SAVED THE DAY, KABAE.
OH, I DIDN'T DO ANYTHING. YOU GIRLS INSPIRE ME. SOON ENOUGH, THAT GLASS CEILING IS GOING TO BREAK AND TON WILL BE BRINGING TEA TO YOUR OFFICE.

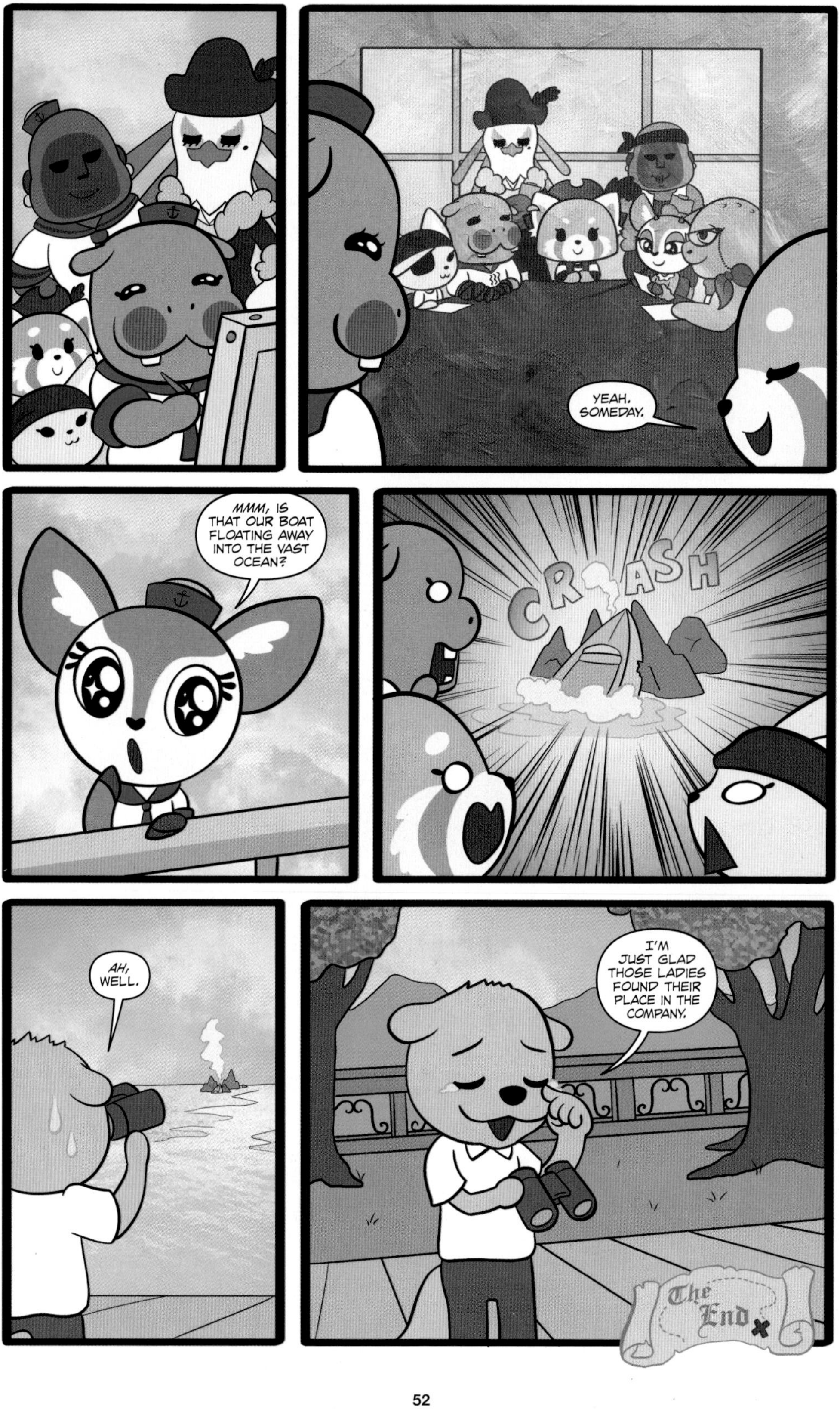
YEAH, SOMEDAY.
MMM, IS THAT OUR BOAT FLOATING AWAY INTO THE VAST OCEAN?
CRASH
AH, WELL.
I'M JUST GLAD THOSE LADIES FOUND THEIR PLACE IN THE COMPANY.
The End

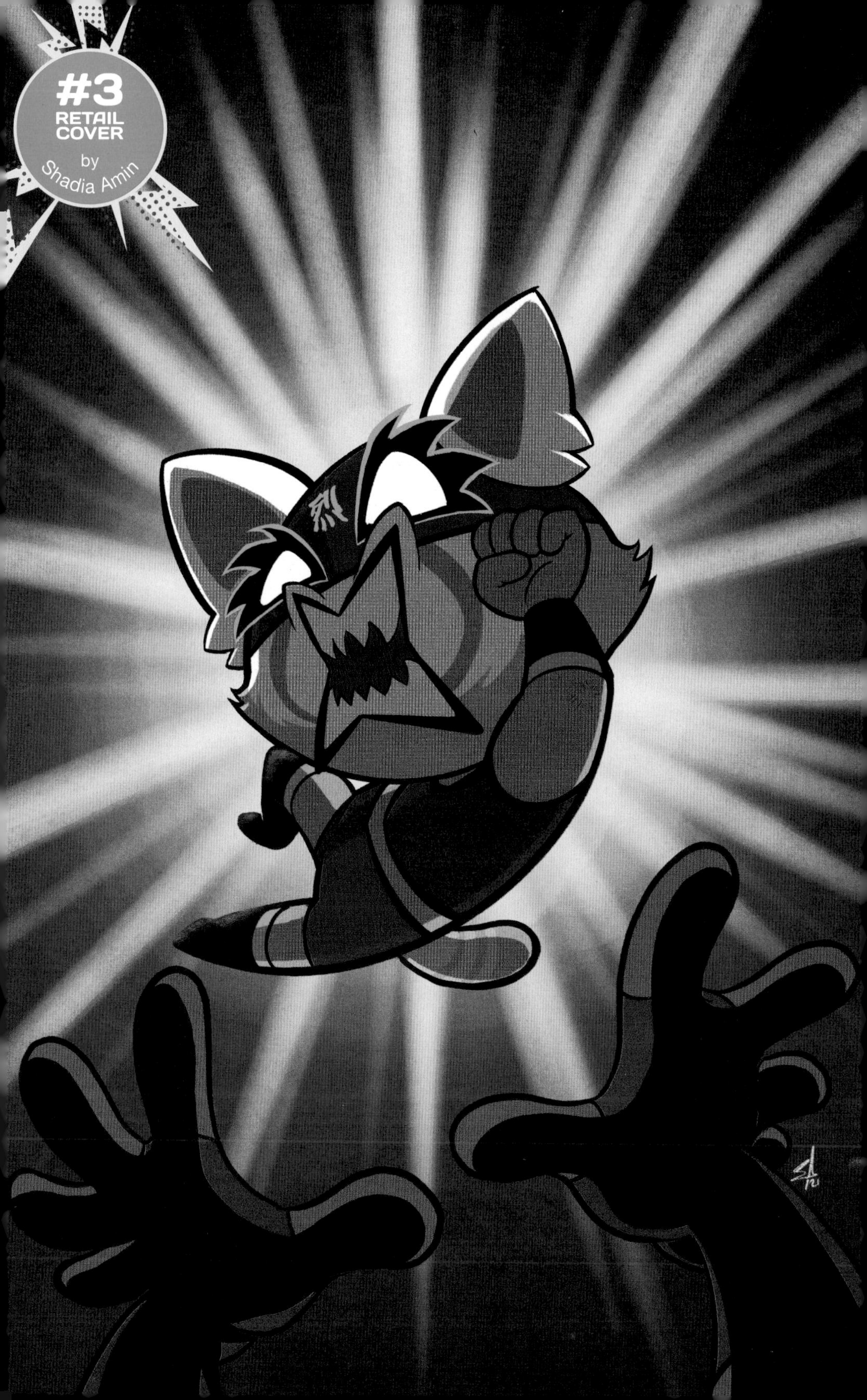
#3
RETAIL
COVER
by
Shadia Amin
烈

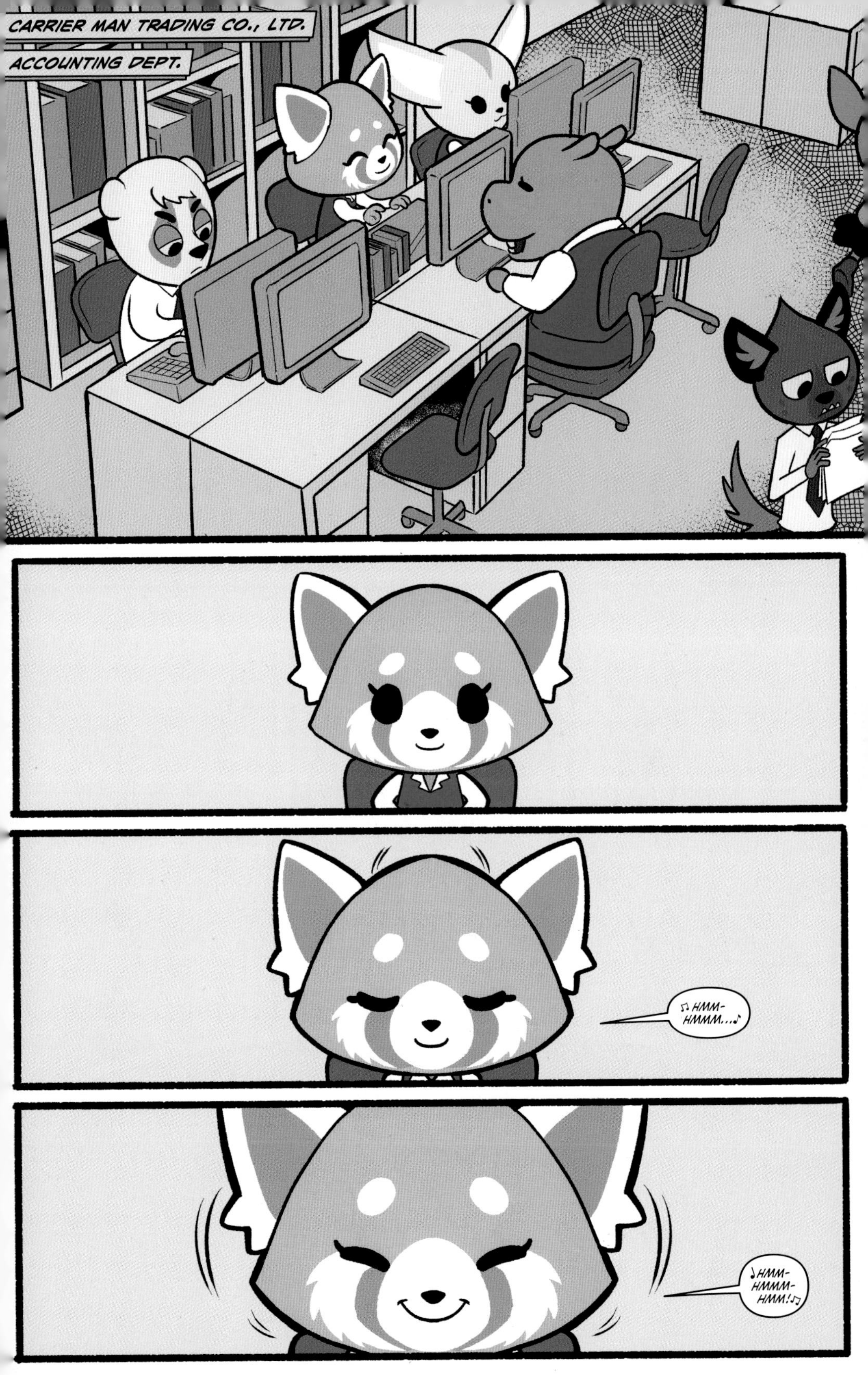
CARRIER MAN TRADING CO., LTD.
ACCOUNTING DEPT.
♫ HMM-HMMM...♪
♪ HMM-HMMM-HMM! ♫

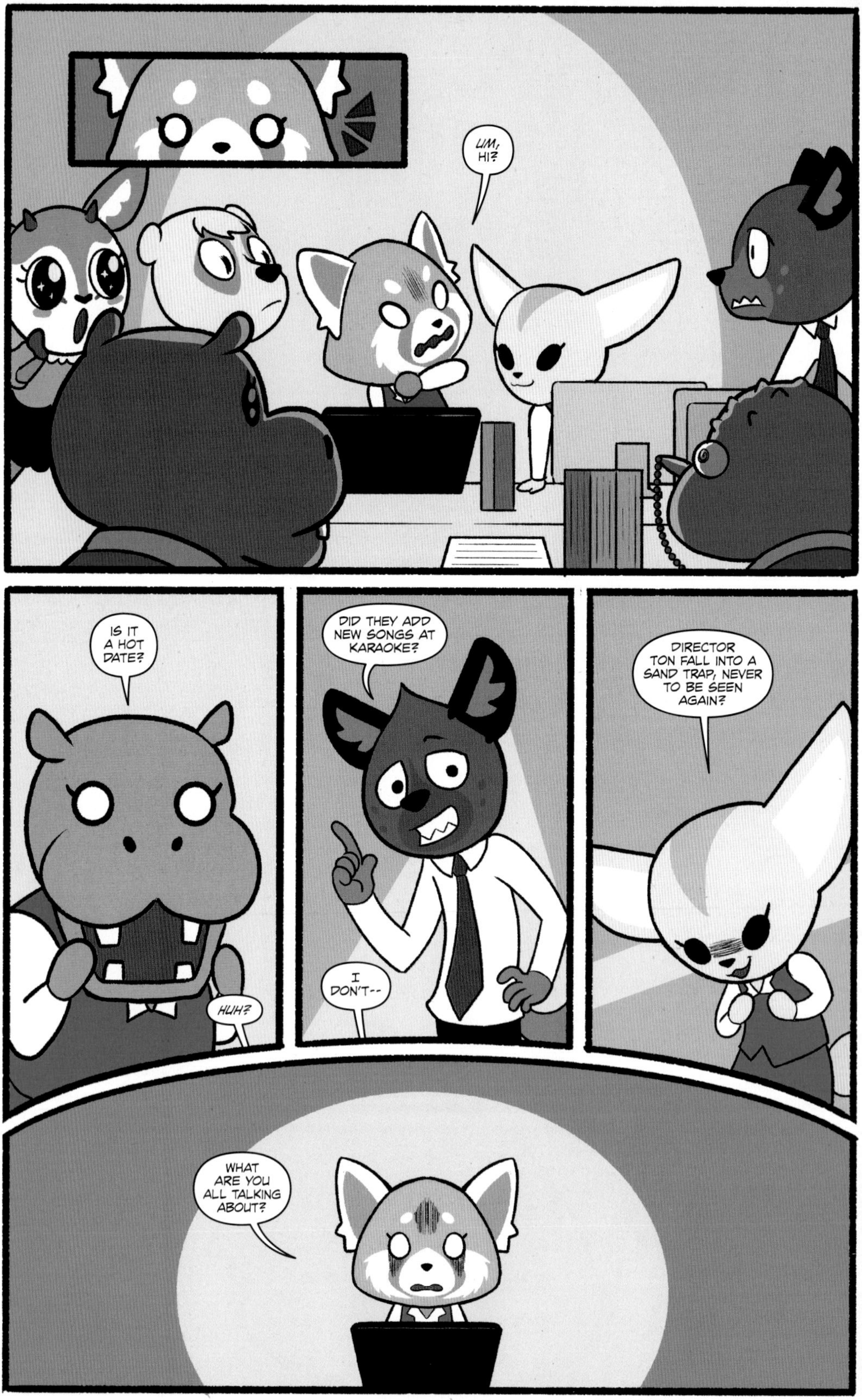
UM, HI?
IS IT A HOT DATE?
HUH?
DID THEY ADD NEW SONGS AT KARAOKE?
I DON'T--
DIRECTOR TON FALL INTO A SAND TRAP, NEVER TO BE SEEN AGAIN?
WHAT ARE YOU ALL TALKING ABOUT?

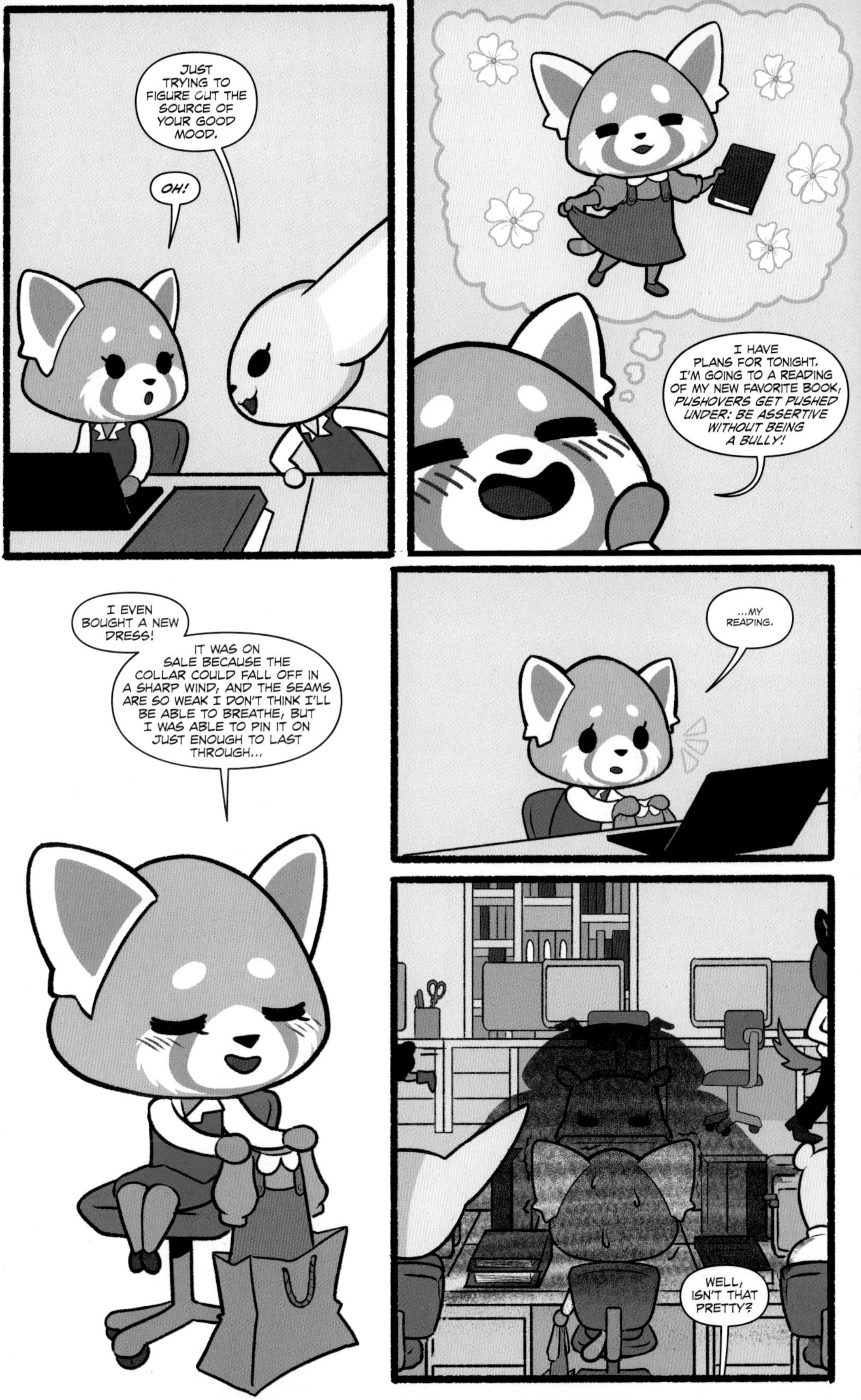
JUST TRYING TO FIGURE OUT THE SOURCE OF YOUR GOOD MOOD.
OH!
I HAVE PLANS FOR TONIGHT. I'M GOING TO A READING OF MY NEW FAVORITE BOOK, *PUSHOVERS GET PUSHED UNDER: BE ASSERTIVE WITHOUT BEING A BULLY!*
I EVEN BOUGHT A NEW DRESS!
IT WAS ON SALE BECAUSE THE COLLAR COULD FALL OFF IN A SHARP WIND, AND THE SEAMS ARE SO WEAK I DON'T THINK I'LL BE ABLE TO BREATHE, BUT I WAS ABLE TO PIN IT ON JUST ENOUGH TO LAST THROUGH...
...MY READING.
WELL, ISN'T THAT PRETTY?

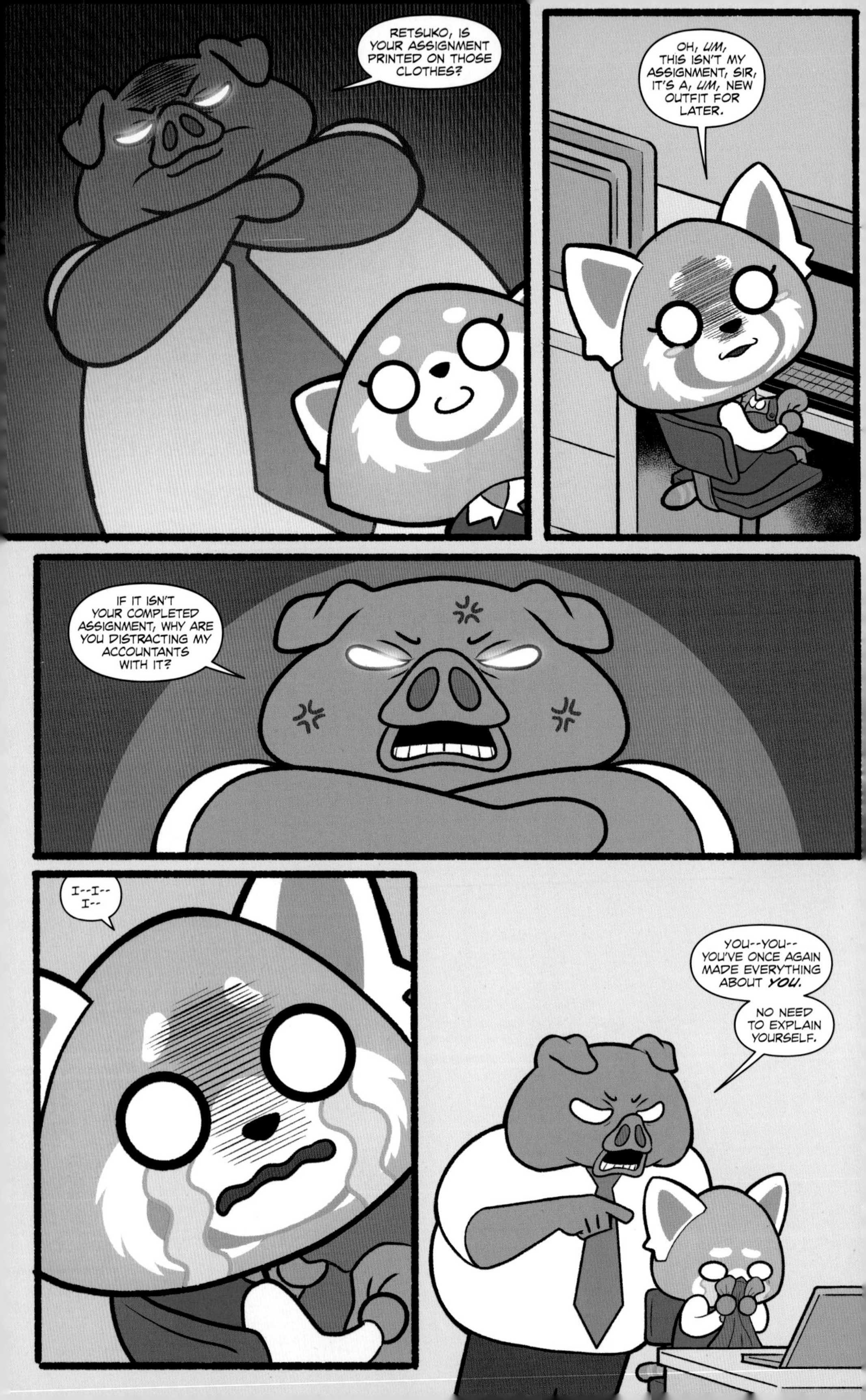
RETSUKO, IS YOUR ASSIGNMENT PRINTED ON THOSE CLOTHES?
OH, *UM*, THIS ISN'T MY ASSIGNMENT, SIR, IT'S A, *UM*, NEW OUTFIT FOR LATER.
IF IT ISN'T YOUR COMPLETED ASSIGNMENT, WHY ARE YOU DISTRACTING MY ACCOUNTANTS WITH IT?
I--I-- I--
YOU--YOU-- YOU'VE ONCE AGAIN MADE EVERYTHING ABOUT ***YOU.***
NO NEED TO EXPLAIN YOURSELF.

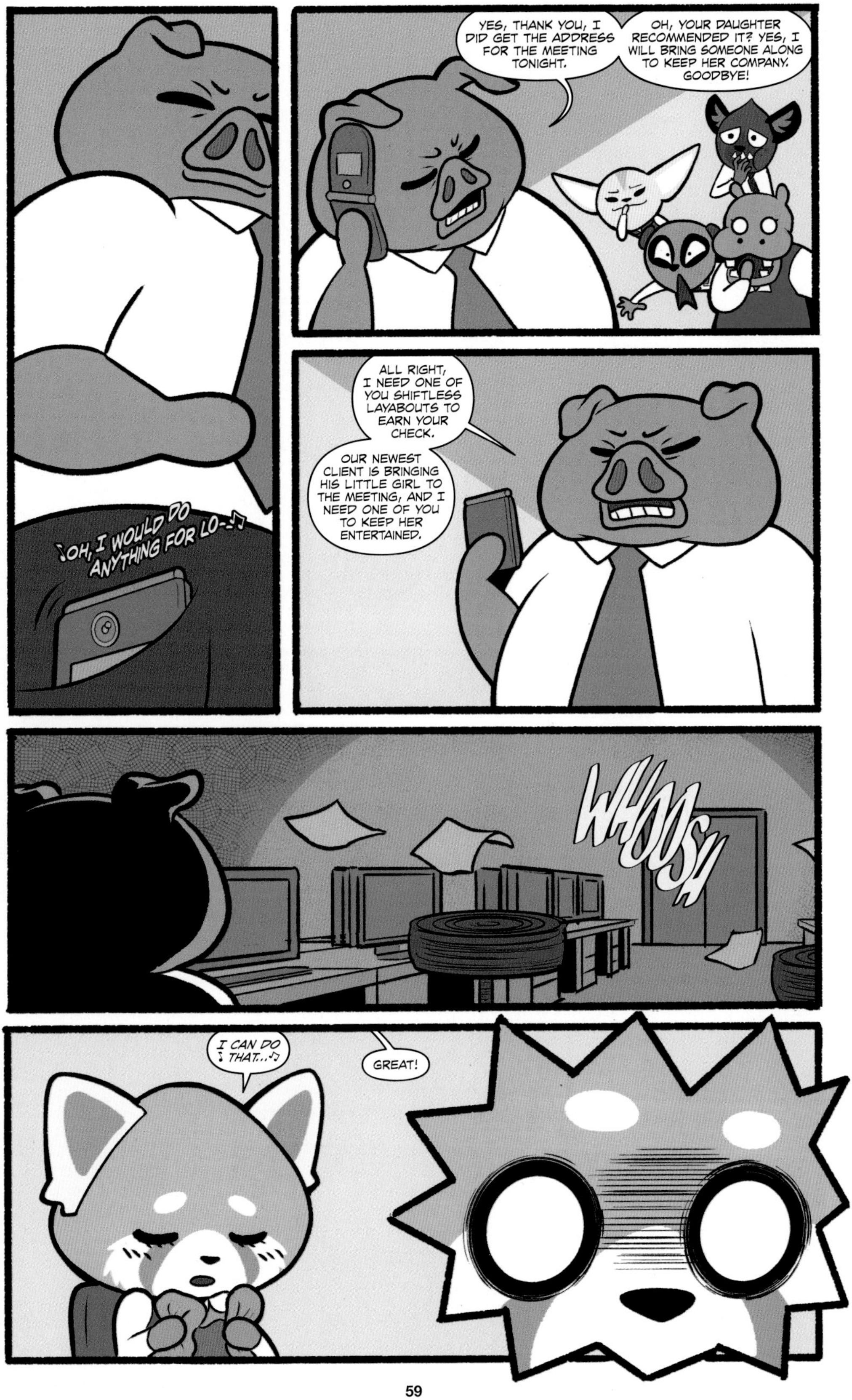
♪OH, I WOULD DO ANYTHING FOR LO-♪♫
YES, THANK YOU, I DID GET THE ADDRESS FOR THE MEETING TONIGHT.
OH, YOUR DAUGHTER RECOMMENDED IT? YES, I WILL BRING SOMEONE ALONG TO KEEP HER COMPANY. GOODBYE!
ALL RIGHT, I NEED ONE OF YOU SHIFTLESS LAYABOUTS TO EARN YOUR CHECK.
OUR NEWEST CLIENT IS BRINGING HIS LITTLE GIRL TO THE MEETING, AND I NEED ONE OF YOU TO KEEP HER ENTERTAINED.
WHOOSH
I CAN DO ♪ THAT...♫
GREAT!

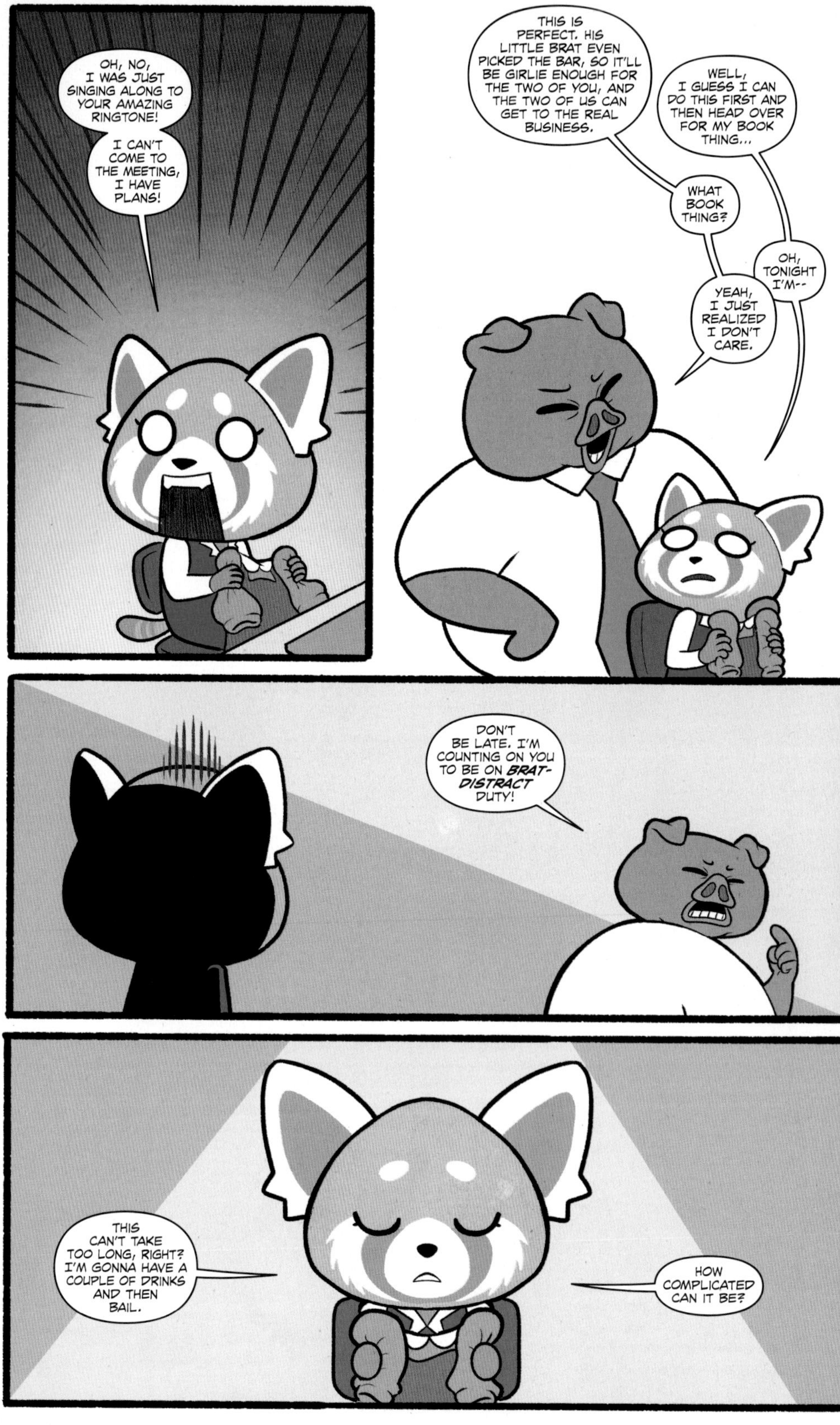

OH, NO, I WAS JUST SINGING ALONG TO YOUR AMAZING RINGTONE!
I CAN'T COME TO THE MEETING, I HAVE PLANS!
THIS IS PERFECT. HIS LITTLE BRAT EVEN PICKED THE BAR, SO IT'LL BE GIRLIE ENOUGH FOR THE TWO OF YOU, AND THE TWO OF US CAN GET TO THE REAL BUSINESS.
WELL, I GUESS I CAN DO THIS FIRST AND THEN HEAD OVER FOR MY BOOK THING...
WHAT BOOK THING?
OH, TONIGHT I'M--
YEAH, I JUST REALIZED I DON'T CARE.
DON'T BE LATE. I'M COUNTING ON YOU TO BE ON BRAT-DISTRACT DUTY!
THIS CAN'T TAKE TOO LONG, RIGHT? I'M GONNA HAVE A COUPLE OF DRINKS AND THEN BAIL.
HOW COMPLICATED CAN IT BE?

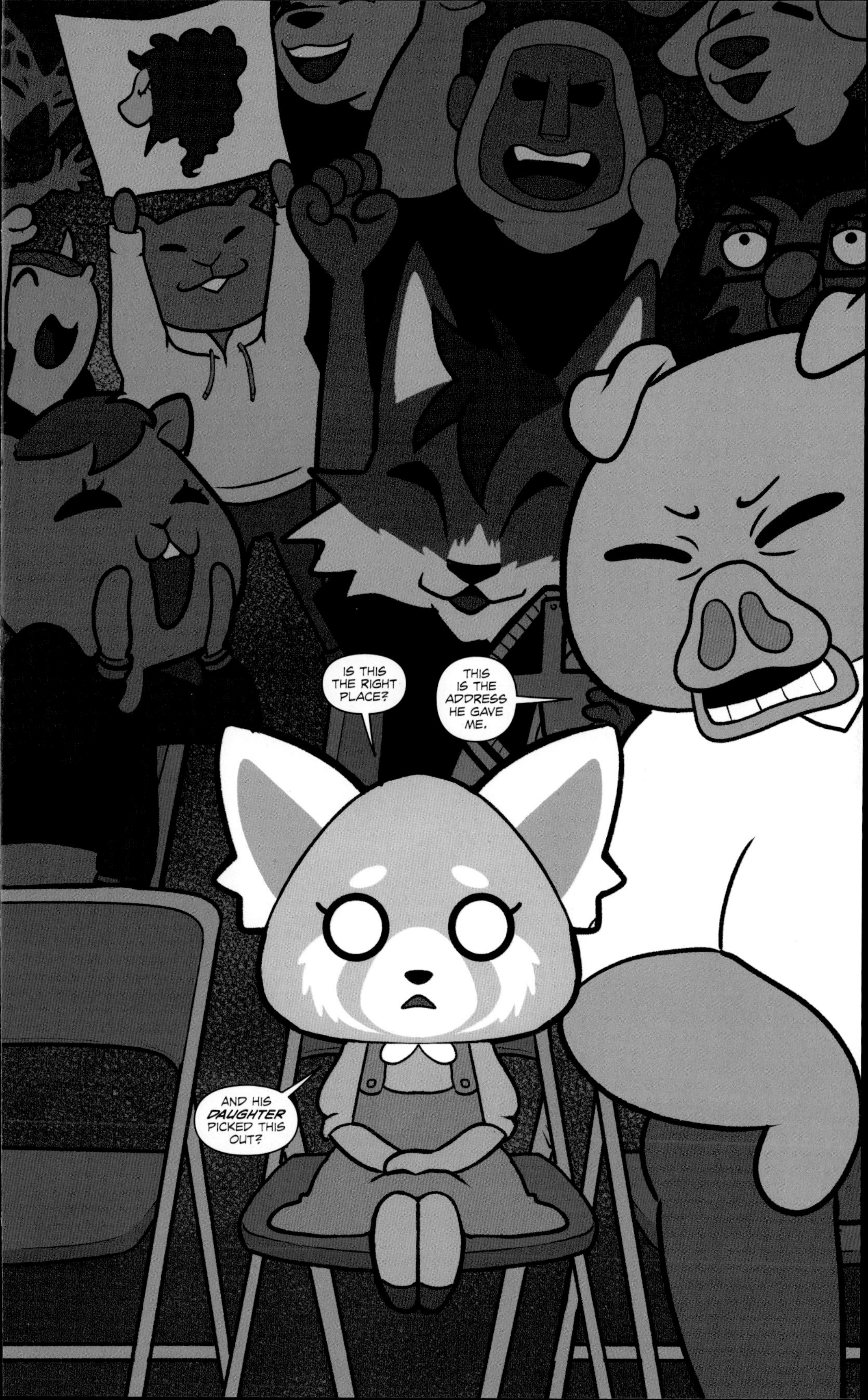
IS THIS THE RIGHT PLACE?
THIS IS THE ADDRESS HE GAVE ME.
AND HIS *DAUGHTER* PICKED THIS OUT?

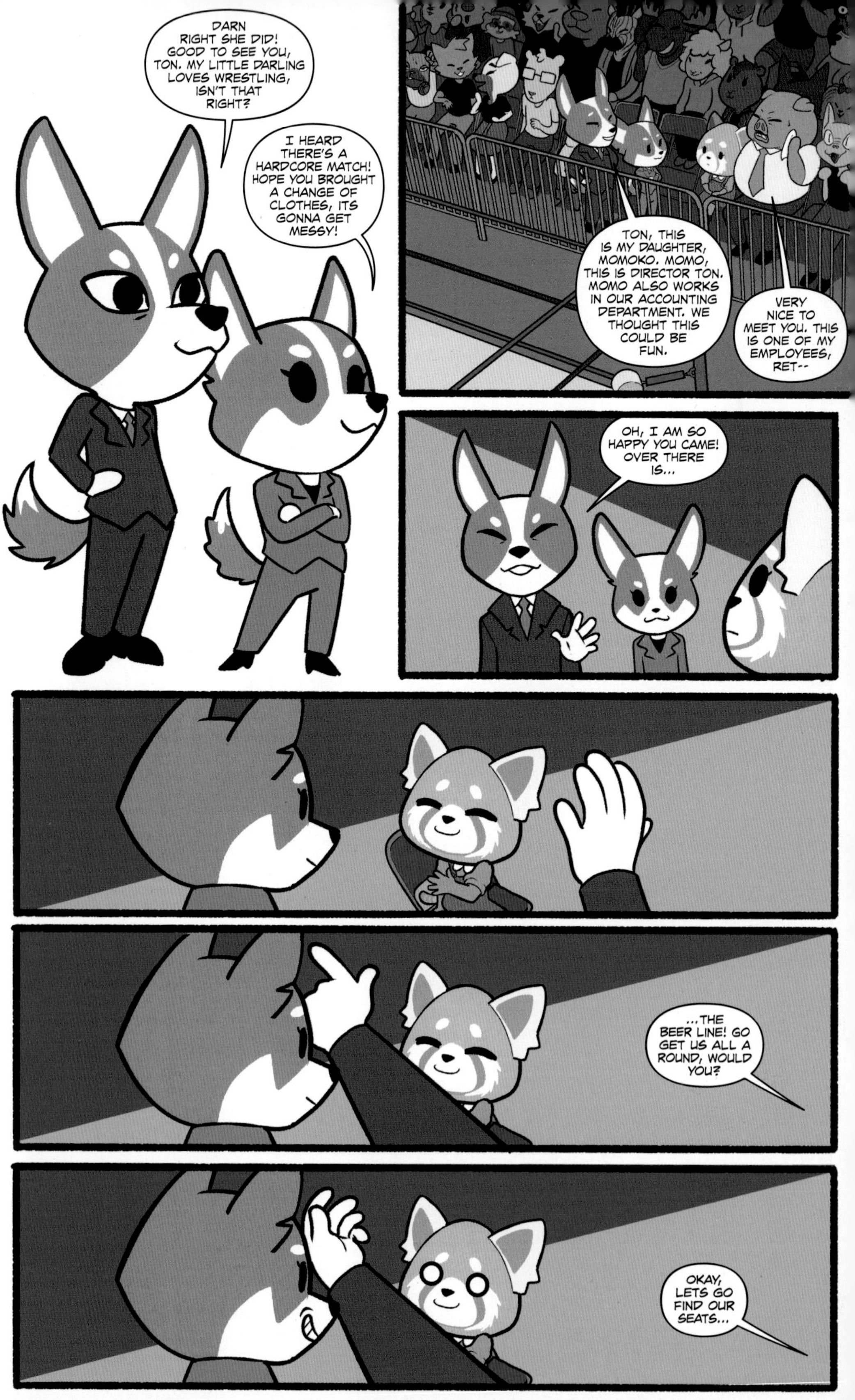

DARN RIGHT SHE DID! GOOD TO SEE YOU, TON. MY LITTLE DARLING LOVES WRESTLING, ISN'T THAT RIGHT?
I HEARD THERE'S A HARDCORE MATCH! HOPE YOU BROUGHT A CHANGE OF CLOTHES, ITS GONNA GET MESSY!
TON, THIS IS MY DAUGHTER, MOMOKO. MOMO, THIS IS DIRECTOR TON. MOMO ALSO WORKS IN OUR ACCOUNTING DEPARTMENT. WE THOUGHT THIS COULD BE FUN.
VERY NICE TO MEET YOU. THIS IS ONE OF MY EMPLOYEES, RET--
OH, I AM SO HAPPY YOU CAME! OVER THERE IS...
...THE BEER LINE! GO GET US ALL A ROUND, WOULD YOU?
OKAY, LETS GO FIND OUR SEATS...

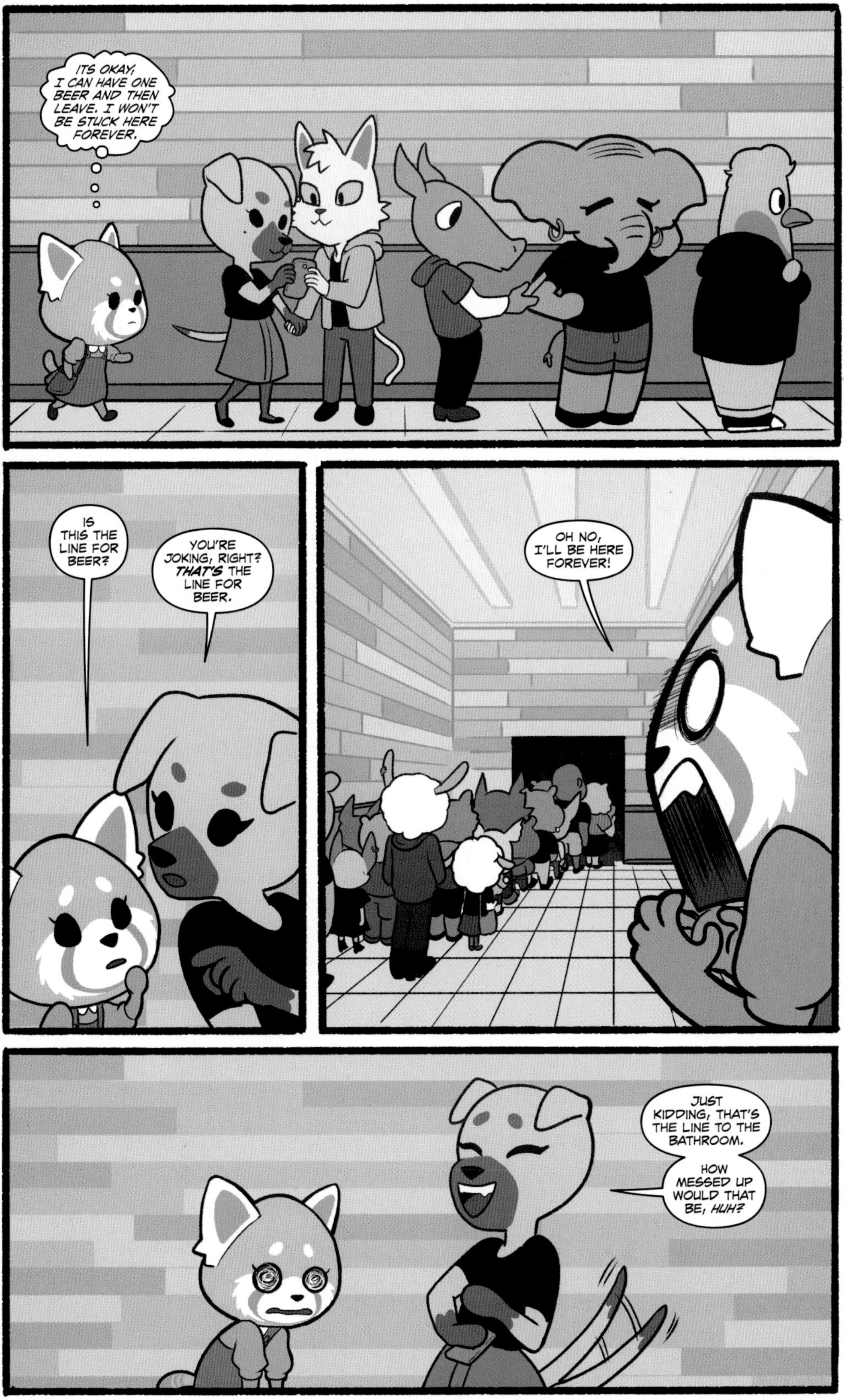
ITS OKAY, I CAN HAVE ONE BEER AND THEN LEAVE. I WON'T BE STUCK HERE FOREVER.
IS THIS THE LINE FOR BEER?
YOU'RE JOKING, RIGHT? THAT'S THE LINE FOR BEER.
OH NO, I'LL BE HERE FOREVER!
JUST KIDDING, THAT'S THE LINE TO THE BATHROOM.
HOW MESSED UP WOULD THAT BE, HUH?

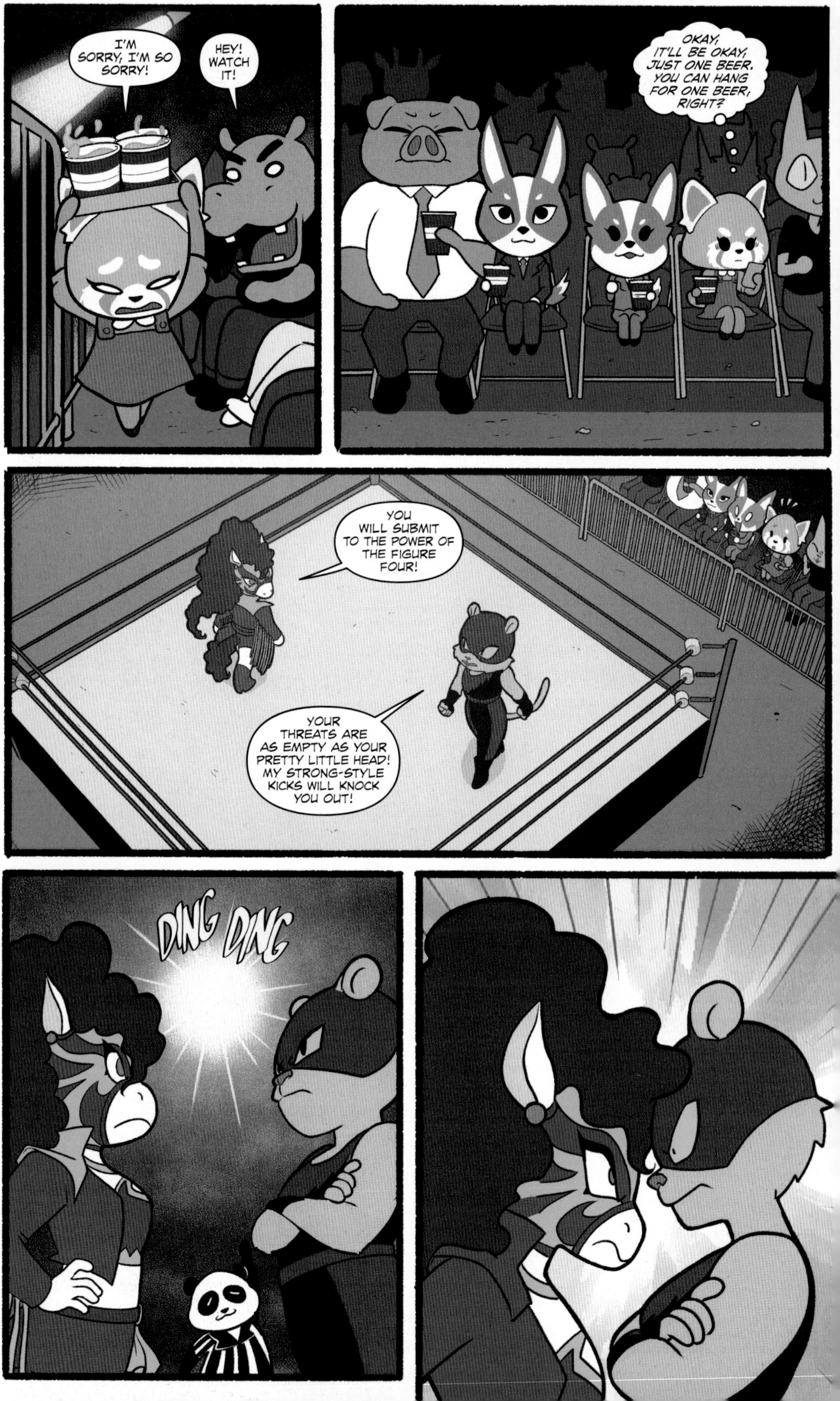
I'M SORRY, I'M SO SORRY!
HEY! WATCH IT!
OKAY, IT'LL BE OKAY, JUST ONE BEER. YOU CAN HANG FOR ONE BEER, RIGHT?
YOU WILL SUBMIT TO THE POWER OF THE FIGURE FOUR!
YOUR THREATS ARE AS EMPTY AS YOUR PRETTY LITTLE HEAD! MY STRONG-STYLE KICKS WILL KNOCK YOU OUT!
DING DING

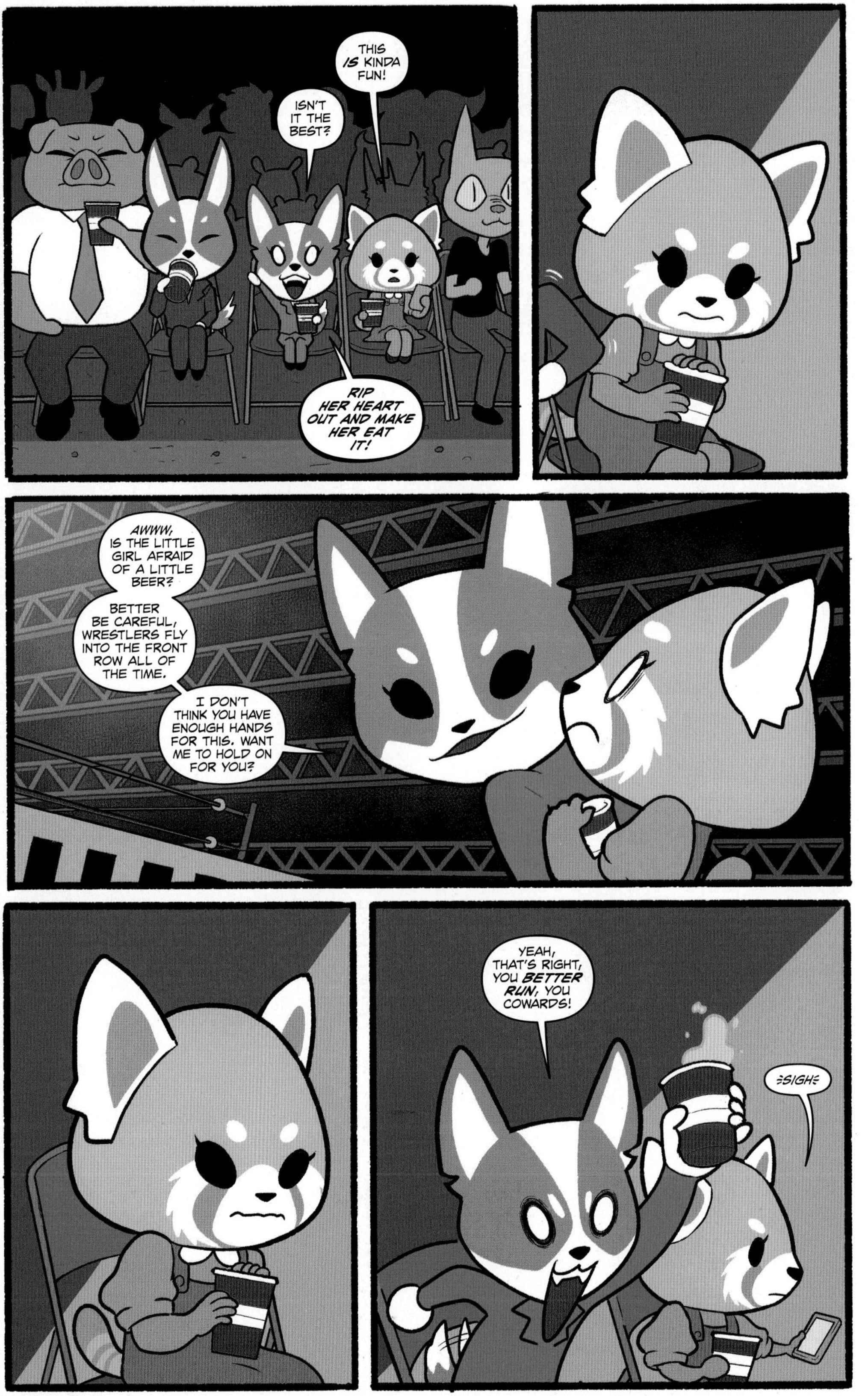
ISN'T IT THE BEST?
THIS IS KINDA FUN!
RIP HER HEART OUT AND MAKE HER EAT IT!
AWWW, IS THE LITTLE GIRL AFRAID OF A LITTLE BEER?
BETTER BE CAREFUL, WRESTLERS FLY INTO THE FRONT ROW ALL OF THE TIME.
I DON'T THINK YOU HAVE ENOUGH HANDS FOR THIS. WANT ME TO HOLD ON FOR YOU?
YEAH, THAT'S RIGHT, YOU BETTER RUN, YOU COWARDS!
SIGH

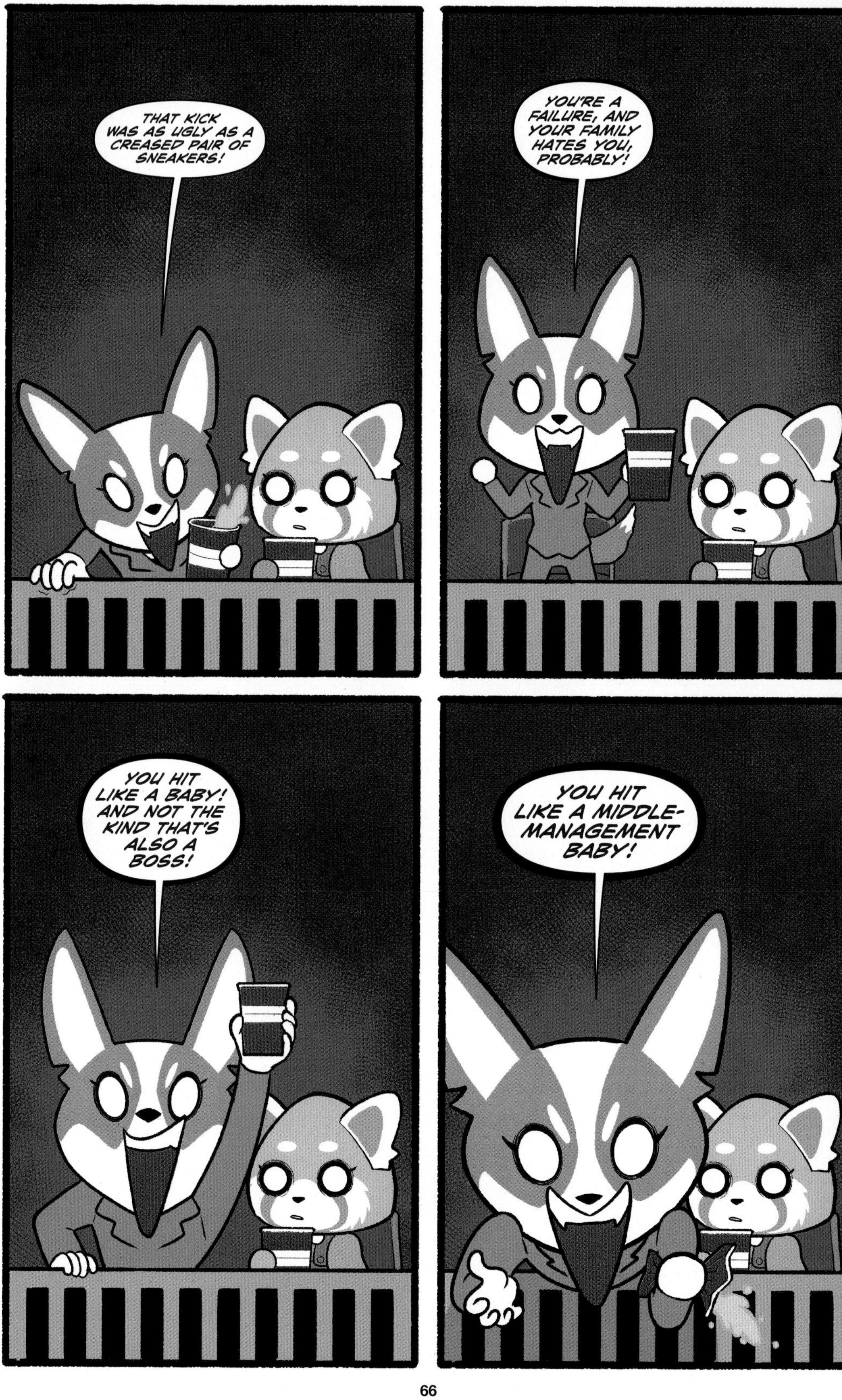
THAT KICK WAS AS UGLY AS A CREASED PAIR OF SNEAKERS!
YOU'RE A FAILURE, AND YOUR FAMILY HATES YOU, PROBABLY!
YOU HIT LIKE A BABY! AND NOT THE KIND THAT'S ALSO A BOSS!
YOU HIT LIKE A MIDDLE-MANAGEMENT BABY!

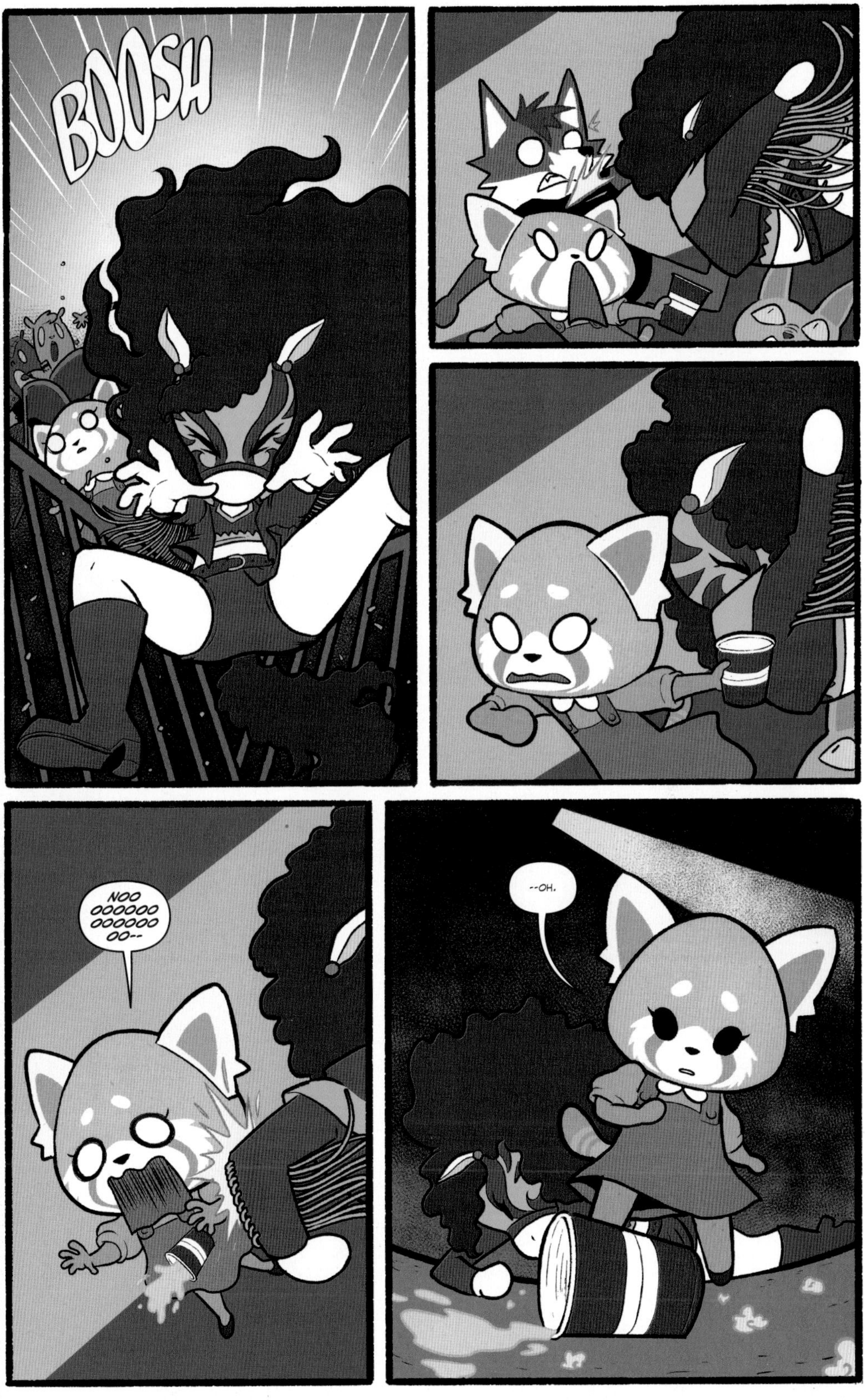
BOOSH
NOO OOOOOO OOOOOO OO--
--OH.

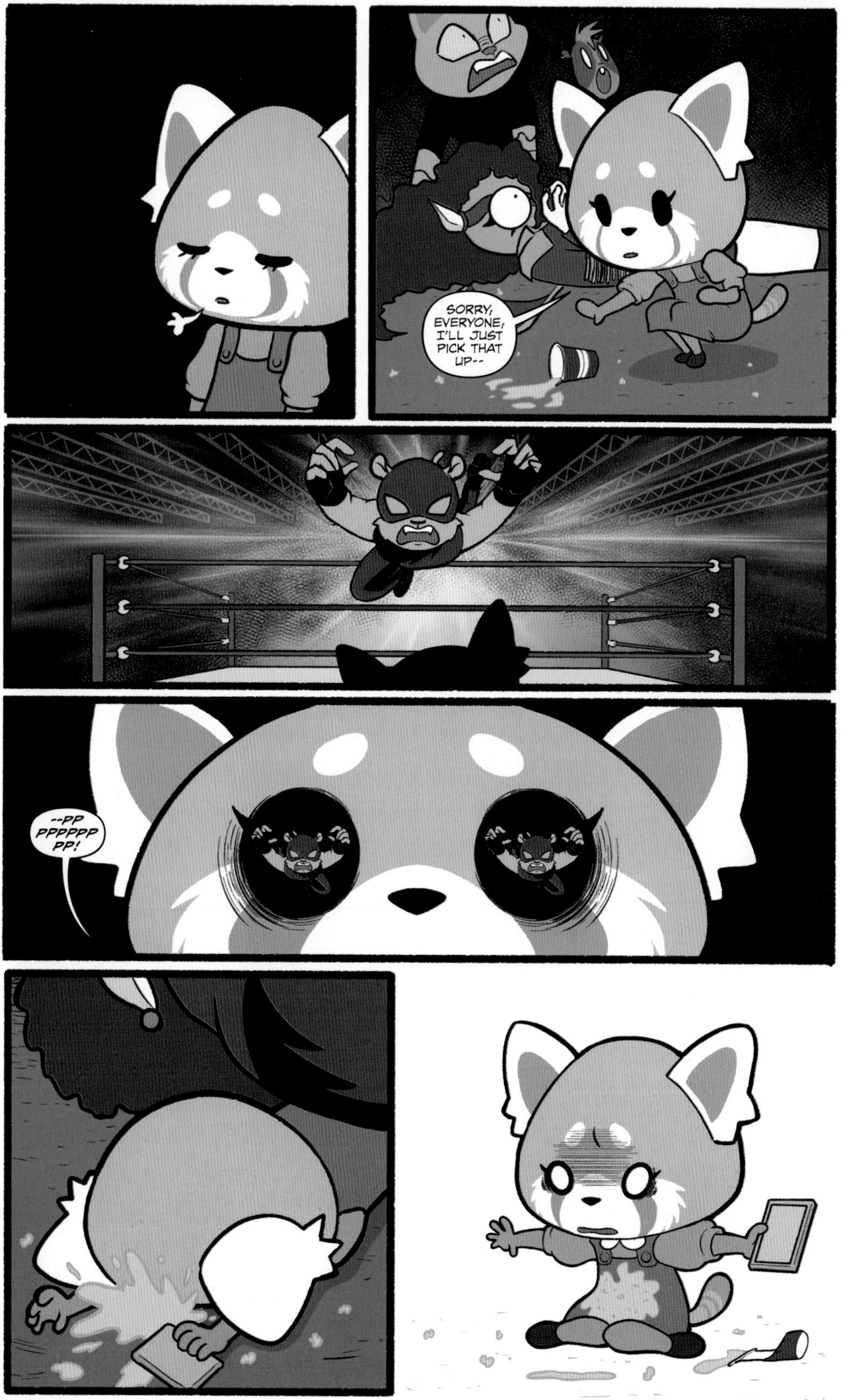
SORRY, EVERYONE, I'LL JUST PICK THAT UP--
--PP PPPPPP PP!

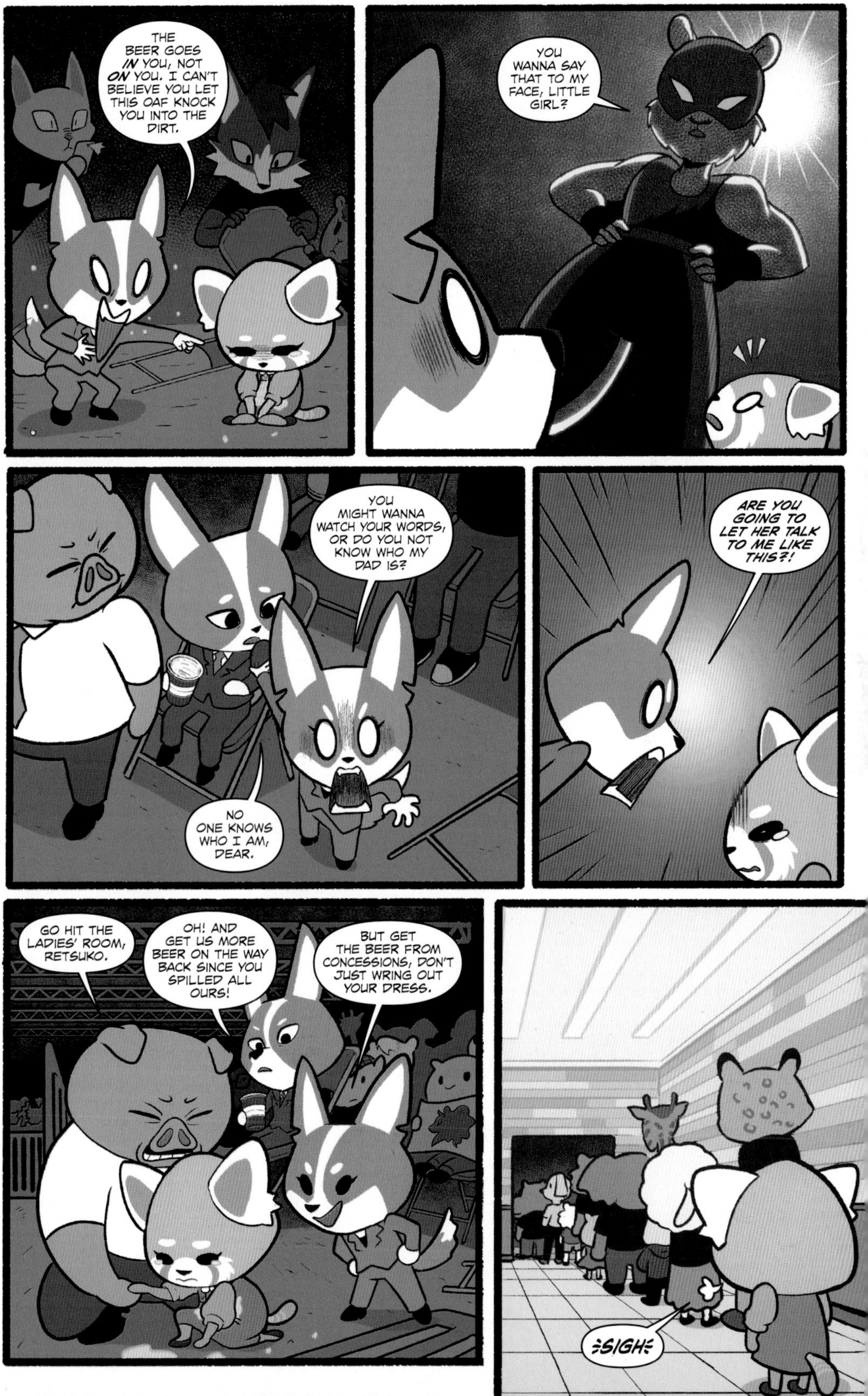
THE BEER GOES IN YOU, NOT ON YOU. I CAN'T BELIEVE YOU LET THIS OAF KNOCK YOU INTO THE DIRT.
YOU WANNA SAY THAT TO MY FACE, LITTLE GIRL?
YOU MIGHT WANNA WATCH YOUR WORDS, OR DO YOU NOT KNOW WHO MY DAD IS?
NO ONE KNOWS WHO I AM, DEAR.
ARE YOU GOING TO LET HER TALK TO ME LIKE THIS?!
GO HIT THE LADIES' ROOM, RETSUKO.
OH! AND GET US MORE BEER ON THE WAY BACK SINCE YOU SPILLED ALL OURS!
BUT GET THE BEER FROM CONCESSIONS, DON'T JUST WRING OUT YOUR DRESS.
SIGH

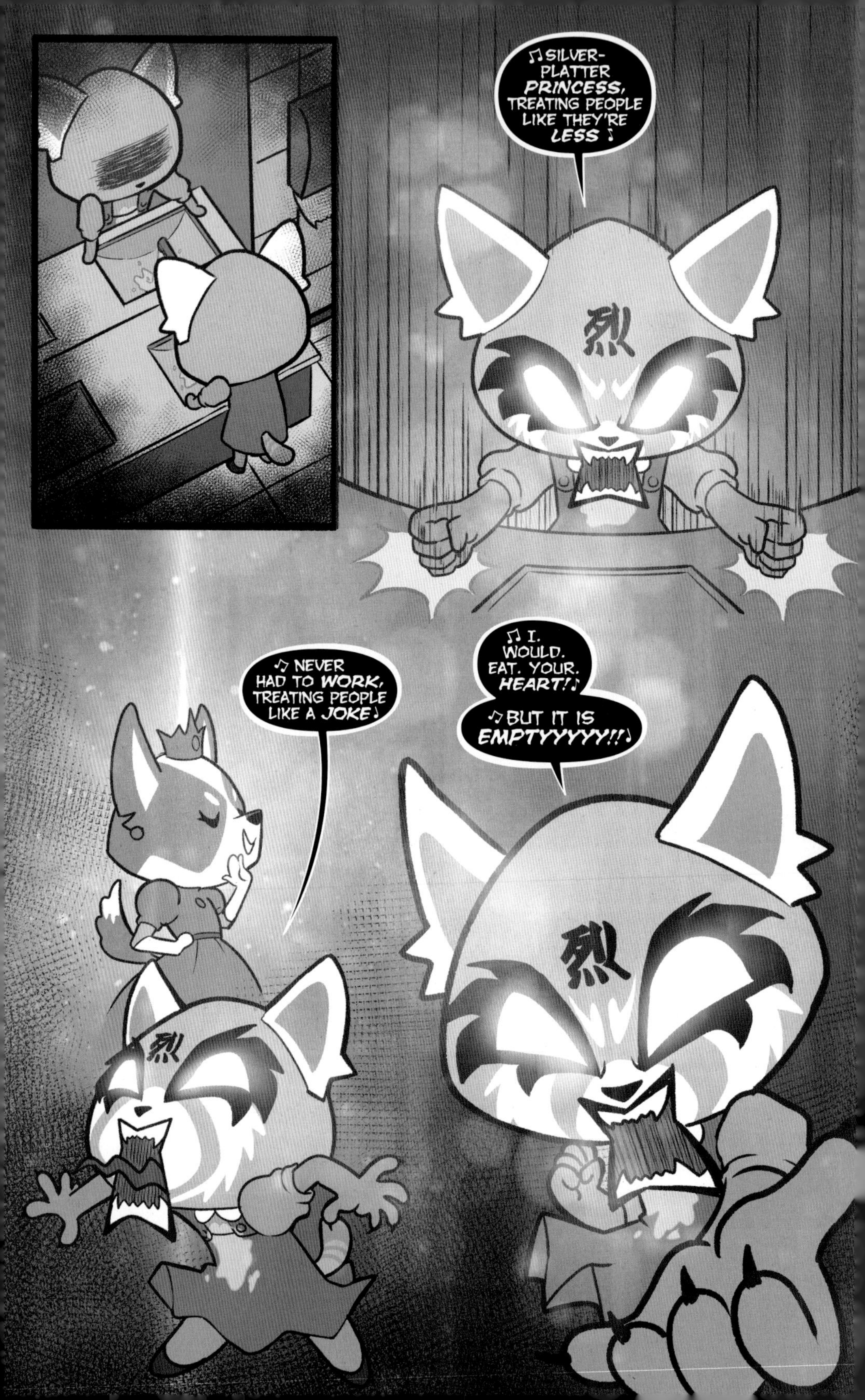
♫ SILVER-PLATTER PRINCESS, TREATING PEOPLE LIKE THEY'RE LESS ♪
♫ NEVER HAD TO WORK, TREATING PEOPLE LIKE A JOKE ♪
♫ I. WOULD. EAT. YOUR. HEART! ♪
♫ BUT IT IS EMPTYYYYY!! ♪

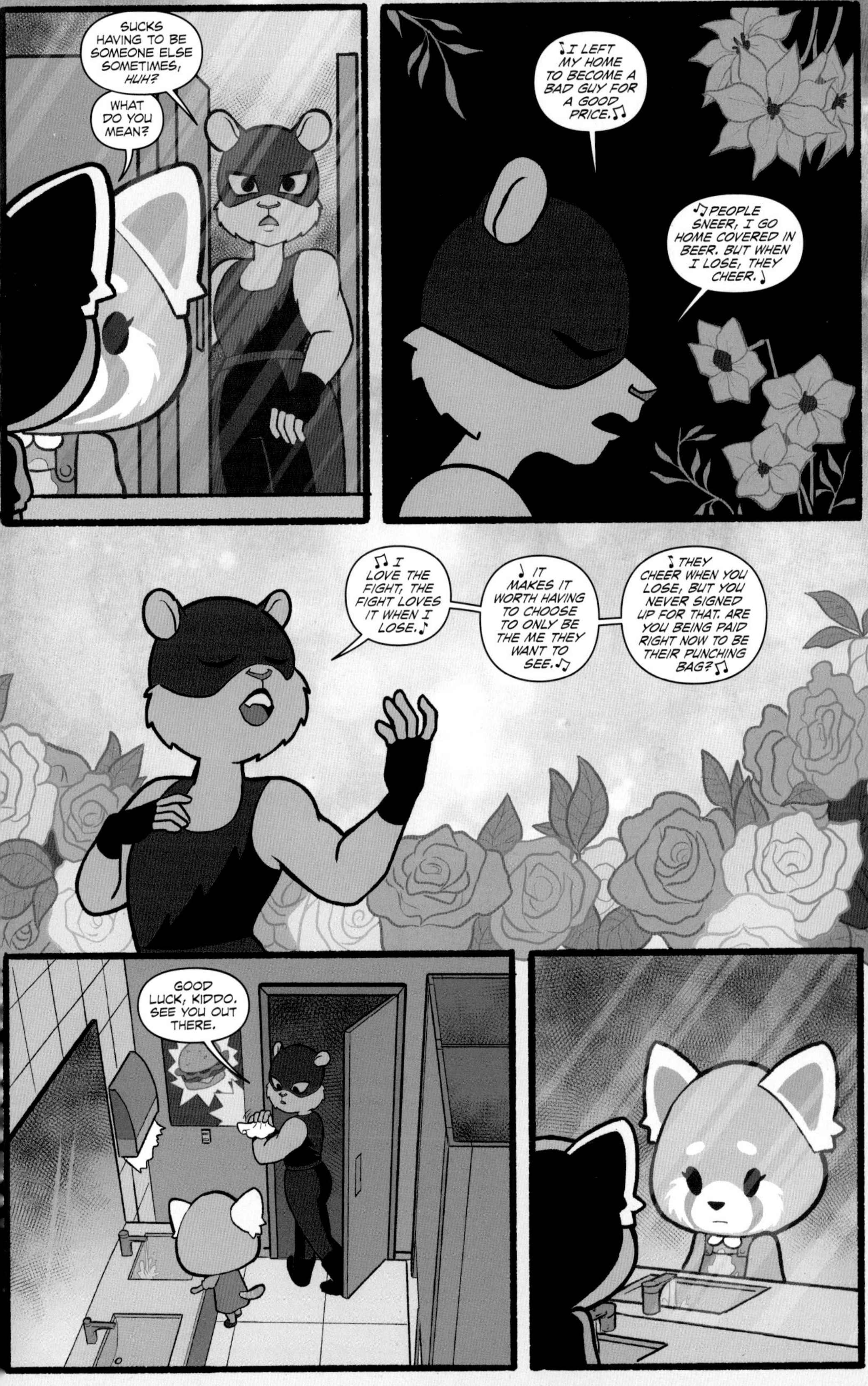
SUCKS HAVING TO BE SOMEONE ELSE SOMETIMES, HUH?
WHAT DO YOU MEAN?
♪I LEFT MY HOME TO BECOME A BAD GUY FOR A GOOD PRICE.♫
♫PEOPLE SNEER, I GO HOME COVERED IN BEER. BUT WHEN I LOSE, THEY CHEER.♪
♫I LOVE THE FIGHT, THE FIGHT LOVES IT WHEN I LOSE.♪
♪IT MAKES IT WORTH HAVING TO CHOOSE TO ONLY BE THE ME THEY WANT TO SEE.♫
♪THEY CHEER WHEN YOU LOSE, BUT YOU NEVER SIGNED UP FOR THAT. ARE YOU BEING PAID RIGHT NOW TO BE THEIR PUNCHING BAG?♫
GOOD LUCK, KIDDO. SEE YOU OUT THERE.

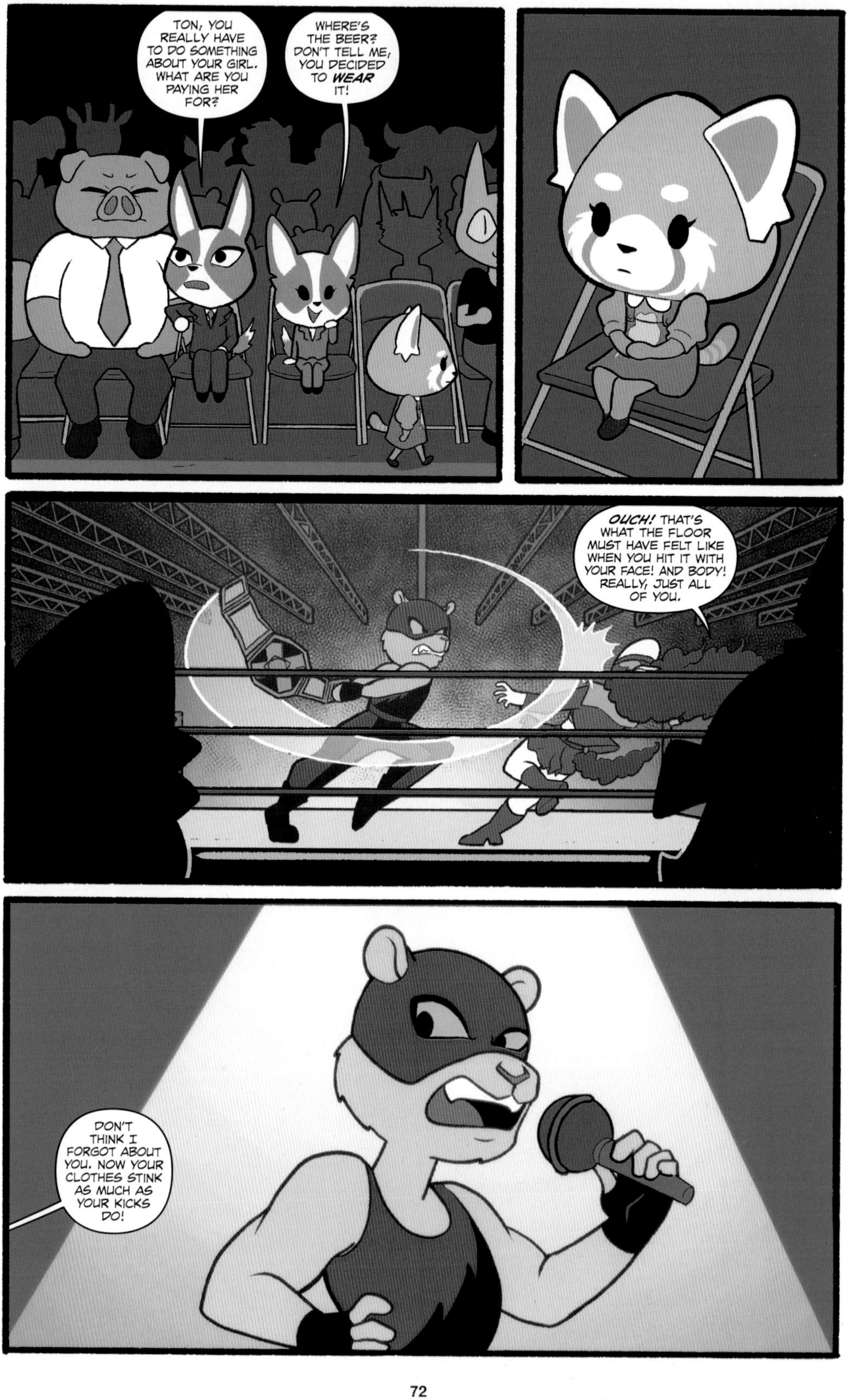
TON, YOU REALLY HAVE TO DO SOMETHING ABOUT YOUR GIRL. WHAT ARE YOU PAYING HER FOR?
WHERE'S THE BEER? DON'T TELL ME, YOU DECIDED TO *WEAR* IT!
OUCH! THAT'S WHAT THE FLOOR MUST HAVE FELT LIKE WHEN YOU HIT IT WITH YOUR FACE! AND BODY! REALLY, JUST ALL OF YOU.
DON'T THINK I FORGOT ABOUT YOU. NOW YOUR CLOTHES STINK AS MUCH AS YOUR KICKS DO!

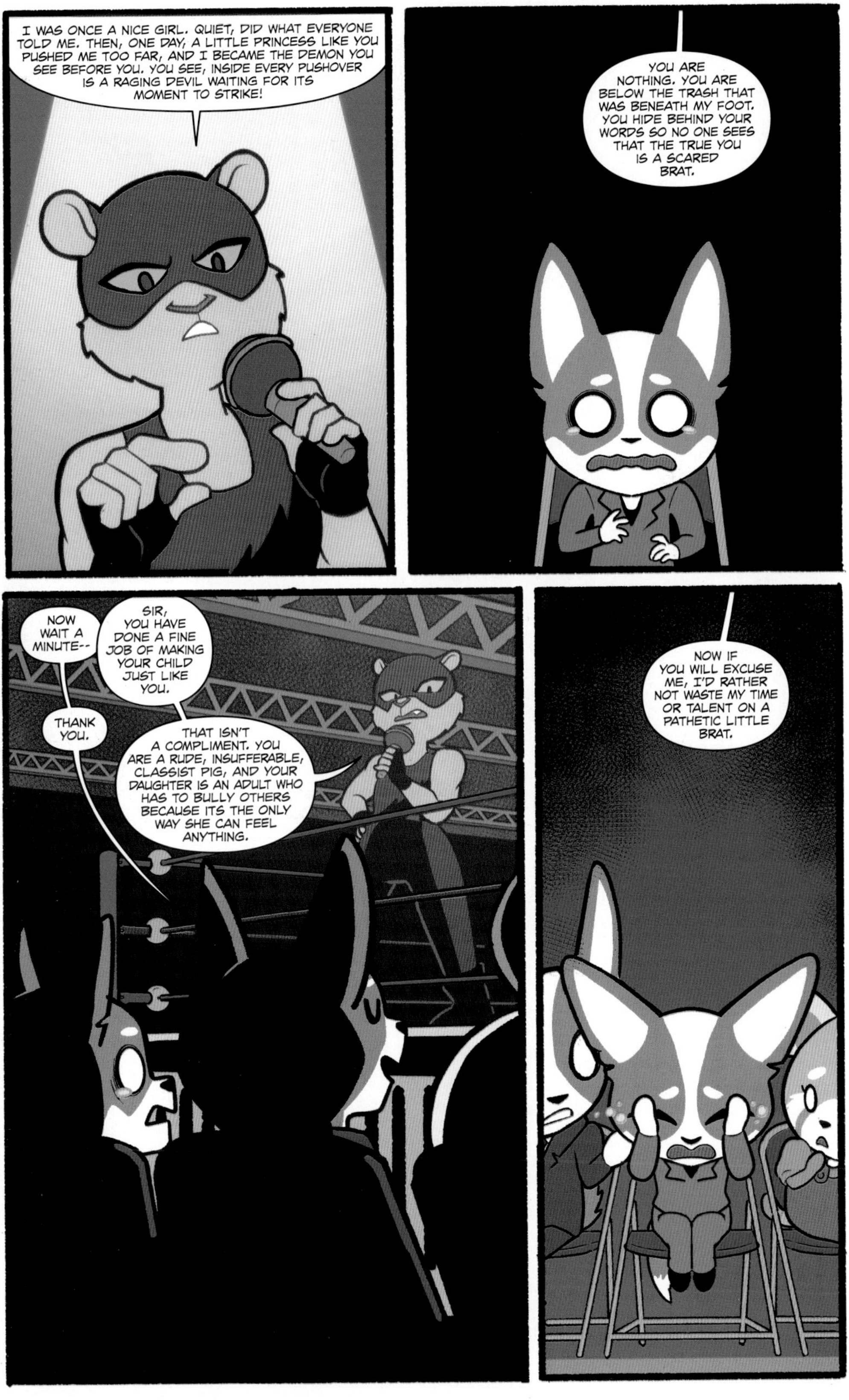
I WAS ONCE A NICE GIRL. QUIET, DID WHAT EVERYONE TOLD ME. THEN, ONE DAY, A LITTLE PRINCESS LIKE YOU PUSHED ME TOO FAR, AND I BECAME THE DEMON YOU SEE BEFORE YOU. YOU SEE, INSIDE EVERY PUSHOVER IS A RAGING DEVIL WAITING FOR ITS MOMENT TO STRIKE!
YOU ARE NOTHING. YOU ARE BELOW THE TRASH THAT WAS BENEATH MY FOOT. YOU HIDE BEHIND YOUR WORDS SO NO ONE SEES THAT THE TRUE YOU IS A SCARED BRAT.
SIR, YOU HAVE DONE A FINE JOB OF MAKING YOUR CHILD JUST LIKE YOU.
THANK YOU.
NOW WAIT A MINUTE--
THAT ISN'T A COMPLIMENT. YOU ARE A RUDE, INSUFFERABLE, CLASSIST PIG, AND YOUR DAUGHTER IS AN ADULT WHO HAS TO BULLY OTHERS BECAUSE ITS THE ONLY WAY SHE CAN FEEL ANYTHING.
NOW IF YOU WILL EXCUSE ME, I'D RATHER NOT WASTE MY TIME OR TALENT ON A PATHETIC LITTLE BRAT.

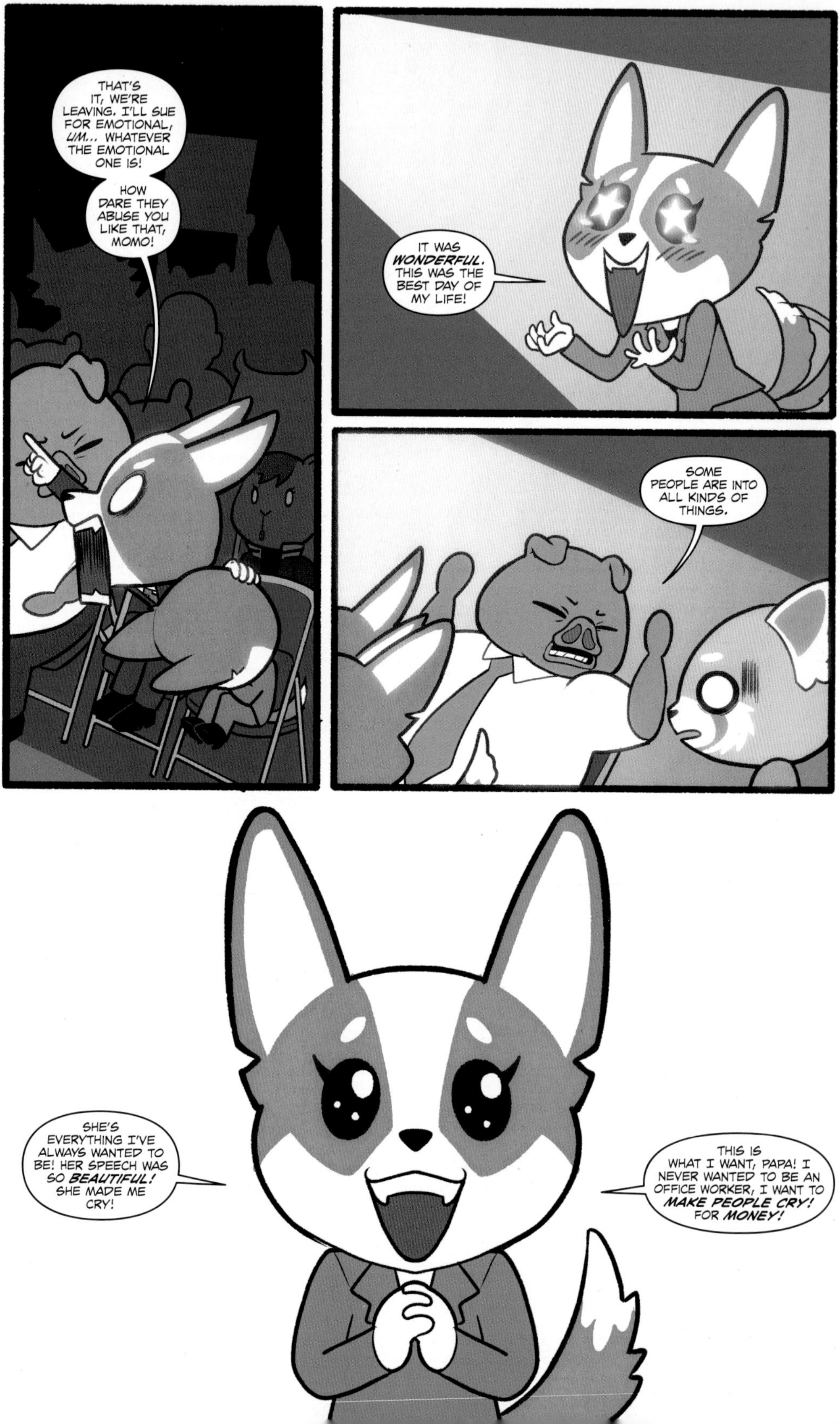
THAT'S IT, WE'RE LEAVING. I'LL SUE FOR EMOTIONAL, *UM...* WHATEVER THE EMOTIONAL ONE IS!
HOW DARE THEY ABUSE YOU LIKE THAT, MOMO!
IT WAS ***WONDERFUL.*** THIS WAS THE BEST DAY OF MY LIFE!
SOME PEOPLE ARE INTO ALL KINDS OF THINGS.
SHE'S EVERYTHING I'VE ALWAYS WANTED TO BE! HER SPEECH WAS SO ***BEAUTIFUL!*** SHE MADE ME CRY!
THIS IS WHAT I WANT, PAPA! I NEVER WANTED TO BE AN OFFICE WORKER, I WANT TO ***MAKE PEOPLE CRY!*** FOR ***MONEY!***

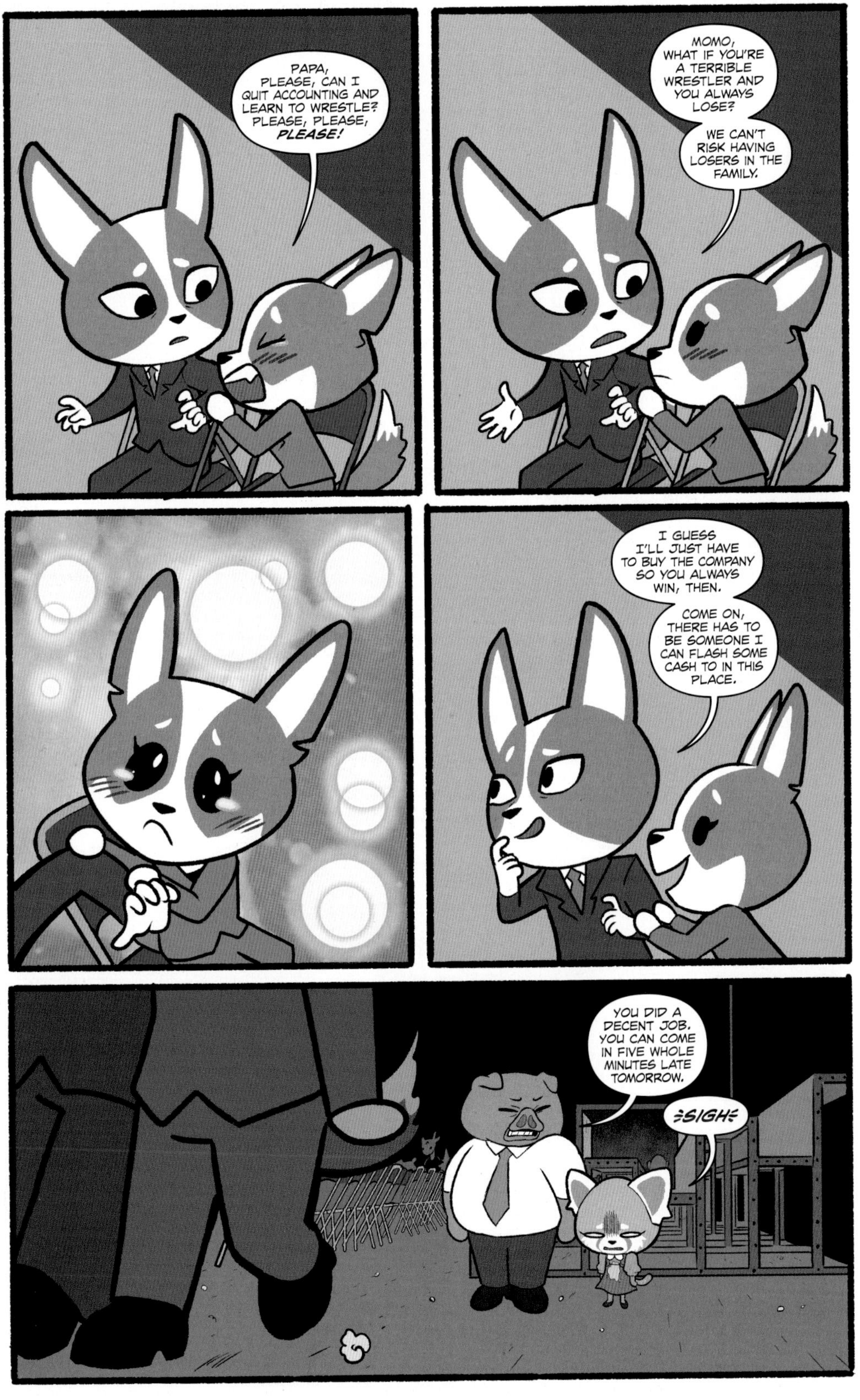
PAPA, PLEASE, CAN I QUIT ACCOUNTING AND LEARN TO WRESTLE? PLEASE, PLEASE, *PLEASE!*
MOMO, WHAT IF YOU'RE A TERRIBLE WRESTLER AND YOU ALWAYS LOSE?
WE CAN'T RISK HAVING LOSERS IN THE FAMILY.
I GUESS I'LL JUST HAVE TO BUY THE COMPANY SO YOU ALWAYS WIN, THEN.
COME ON, THERE HAS TO BE SOMEONE I CAN FLASH SOME CASH TO IN THIS PLACE.
YOU DID A DECENT JOB. YOU CAN COME IN FIVE WHOLE MINUTES LATE TOMORROW.
SIGH

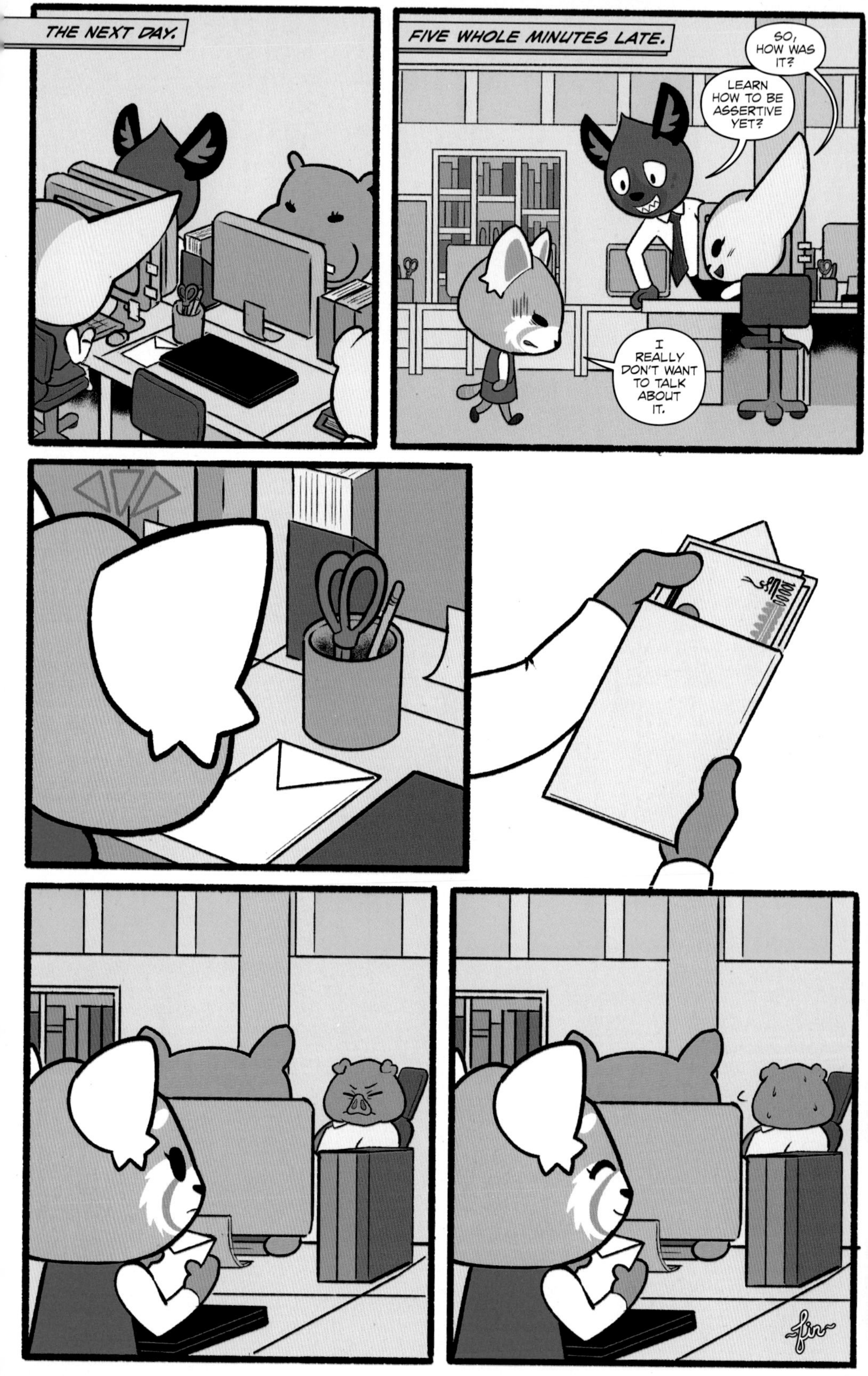
THE NEXT DAY.
FIVE WHOLE MINUTES LATE.
SO, HOW WAS IT?
LEARN HOW TO BE ASSERTIVE YET?
I REALLY DON'T WANT TO TALK ABOUT IT.
-fin-

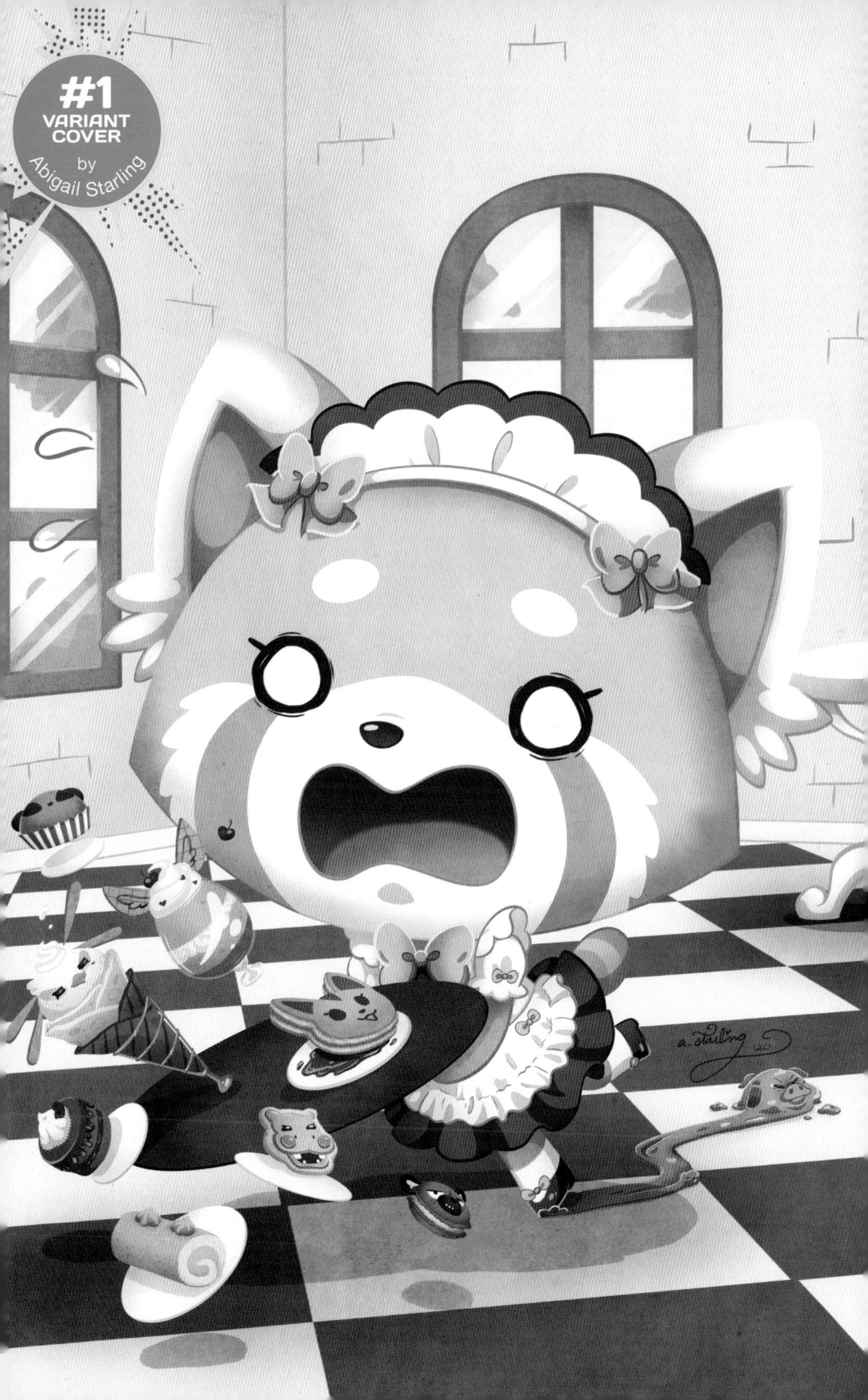
#1
VARIANT
COVER
by
Abigail Starling
a. starling '20

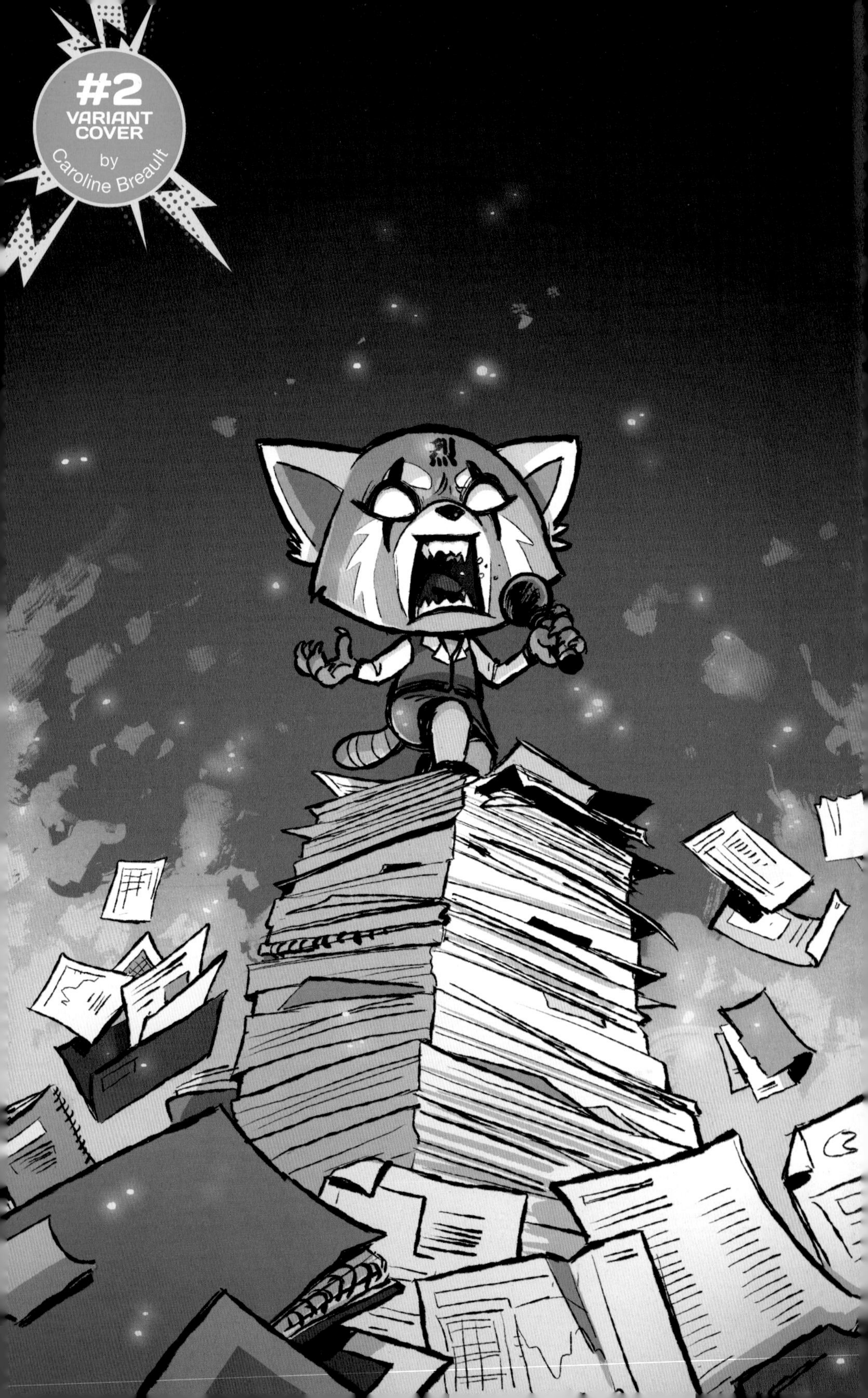
#2
VARIANT
COVER
by
Caroline Breault

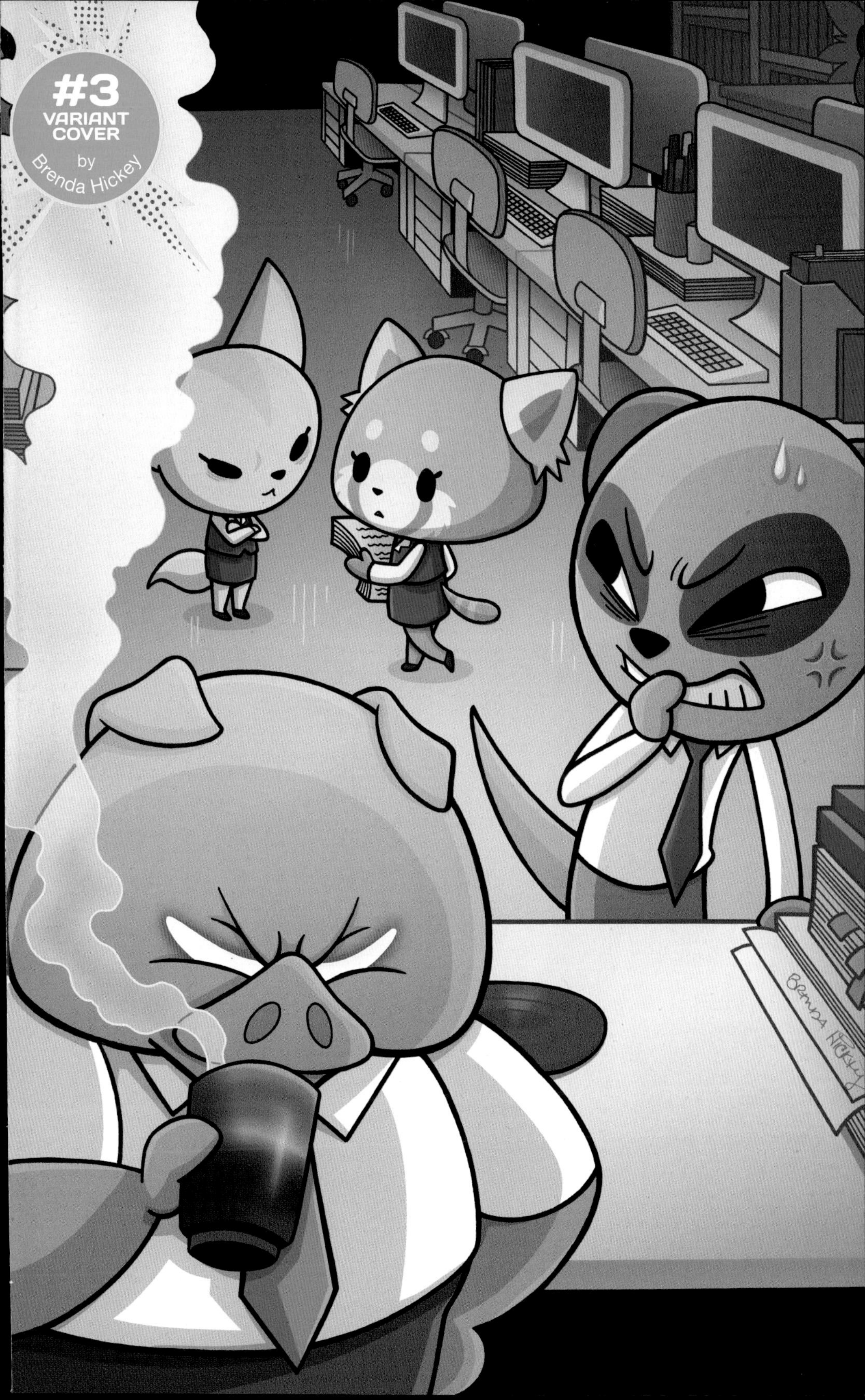
#3
VARIANT
COVER
by
Brenda Hickey

READ MORE FROM ONI PRESS!

Aggretsuko
Little Rei of Sunshine

AGGRETSUKO: LITTLE REI OF SUNSHINE

By Brenda Hickey

Aggretsuko in her first original graphic novel! The office queen of karaoke meets her match when Retsuko's favorite band reunites for a special concert.

Aggretsuko
meet her friends

AGGRETSUKO: MEET HER FRIENDS

By Various

You've come to love Aggretsuko, now get to know her friends in this hardcover collection of the fan-favorite miniseries. This fun and fanciful book puts the spotlight on The Yoga Instructor, Fenneko, and Mr. Ton in three standalone stories.

gudetama
adulting for the lazy
APPLICATION
RESUME
DUE: NOW

GUDETAMA: ADULTING FOR THE LAZY

By Wook-Jin Clark

Adulting is tough. Thankfully, Gudetama is here to guide you on your path to growth!

"Mooncakes is spellbinding!"
–Tillie Walden, Eisner-winning creator of Spinning and On a Sunbeam
Mooncakes
Wendy Xu
Suzanne Walker

MOONCAKES

By Suzanne Walker and Wendy Xu

A story of love and demons, family and witchcraft.

The Black Mage
Daniel Barnes • D.J. Kirkland

THE BLACK MAGE

By Daniel Barnes and D.J. Kirkland

When a historically white wizarding school opens its doors to its first-ever black student, everyone believes that the wizarding community is finally taking its first crucial steps toward inclusivity. Or is it?

GIRL HAVEN

GIRL HAVEN

By Lilah Sturges and Meaghan Carter

Three years ago, Ash's mom, Kristin, left home and never came back. Now, Ash lives in the house where Kristin grew up. All of her things are there. Her old room, her old clothes, and the shed where she spent her childhood creating a fantasy world called Koretris.

For more information on these and other fine Oni Press comic books and graphic novels, visit www.onipress.com.

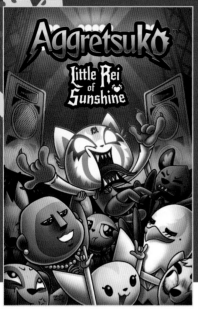

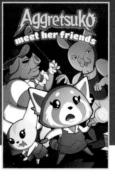

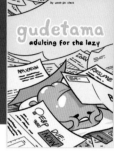

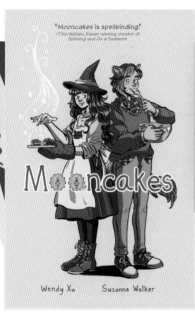

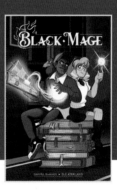

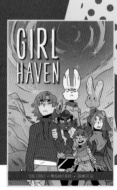

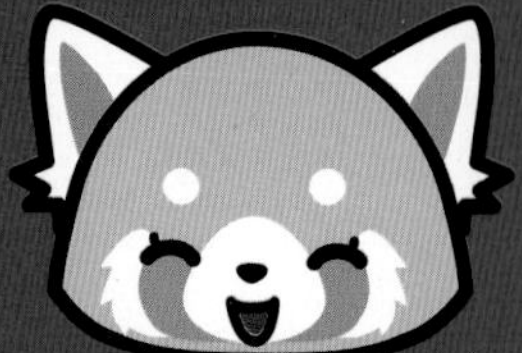